FRANKLIN PARK PUBLIC LIBRARY

FRANKLIN PARK, IL.

Each borrower is held responsible for all library material drawn on his card and for fines accruing on the same. No material will be issued until such fine has been paid.

All injuries to library material beyond reasonable wear and all losses shall be made good to the satisfaction of the Librarian.

Replacement costs will be billed after 42 days overdue.

NOODLEHEADS FIND SOMETHING FISHY

by Tedd Arnold
Martha Hamilton
and Mitch Weiss

illustrated by Tedd Arnold

Holiday House   New York

In memory of Tackle Box Charlie
—T. A.

For Mollie and Alexandra, charter
members of the Noodlehead Club
—M. H. and M. W.

Text copyright © 2018 by Tedd Arnold, Martha Hamilton, and Mitch Weiss
Illustrations copyright © 2018 by Tedd Arnold
All Rights Reserved
HOLIDAY HOUSE is registered in the U.S. Patent and Trademark Office.
Printed and Bound in May 2018 at Toppan Leefung, DongGuan City, China.
The artwork was rendered digitally using Photoshop software.
www.holidayhouse.com
First Edition
1 3 5 7 9 10 8 6 4 2

Library of Congress Cataloging-in-Publication Data is available.

ISBN 978-0-8234-3937-9 (hardcover)

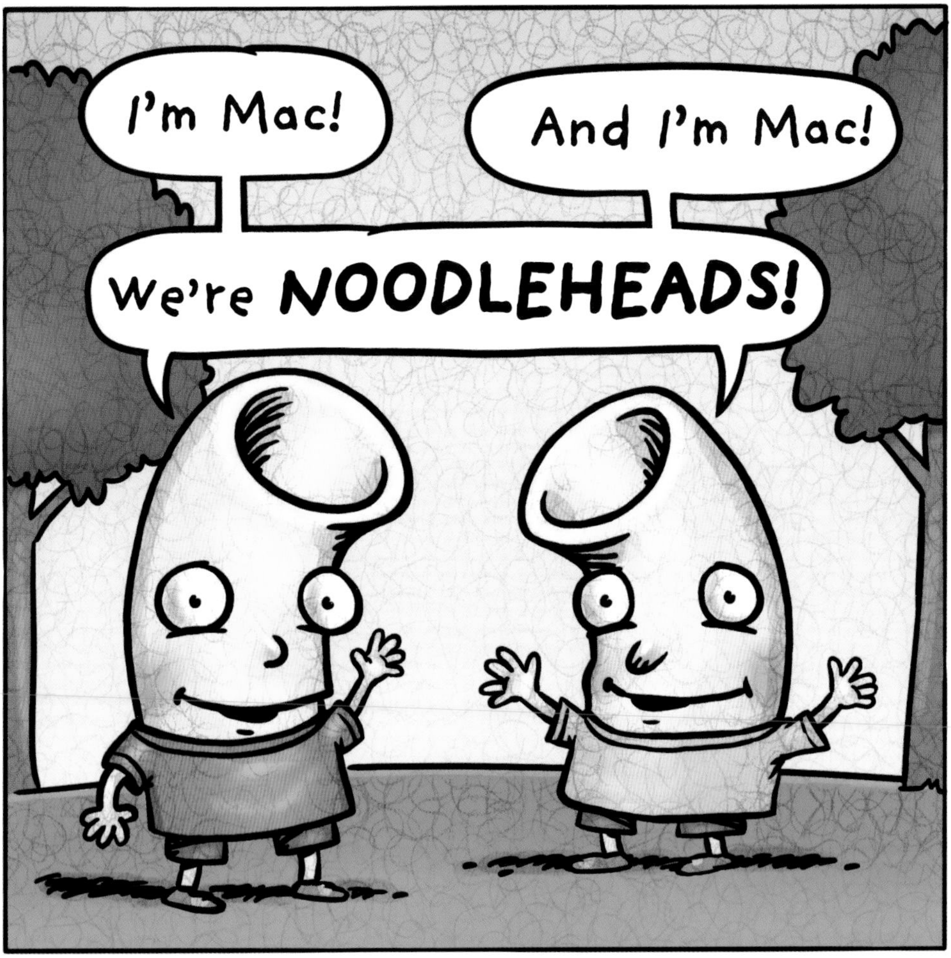
I'm Mac!
And I'm Mac!
We're NOODLEHEADS!

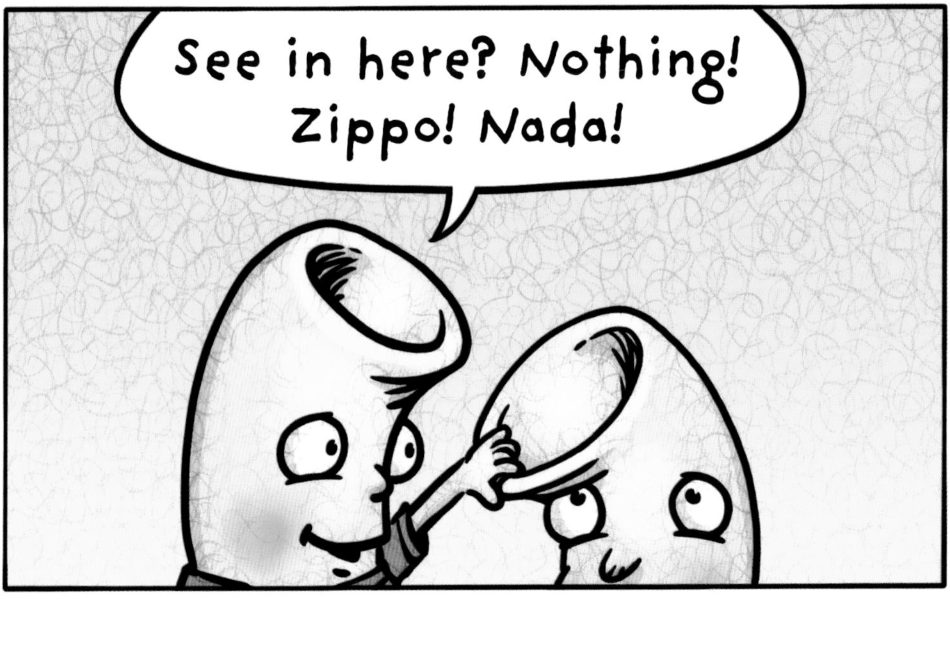
See in here? Nothing!
Zippo! Nada!

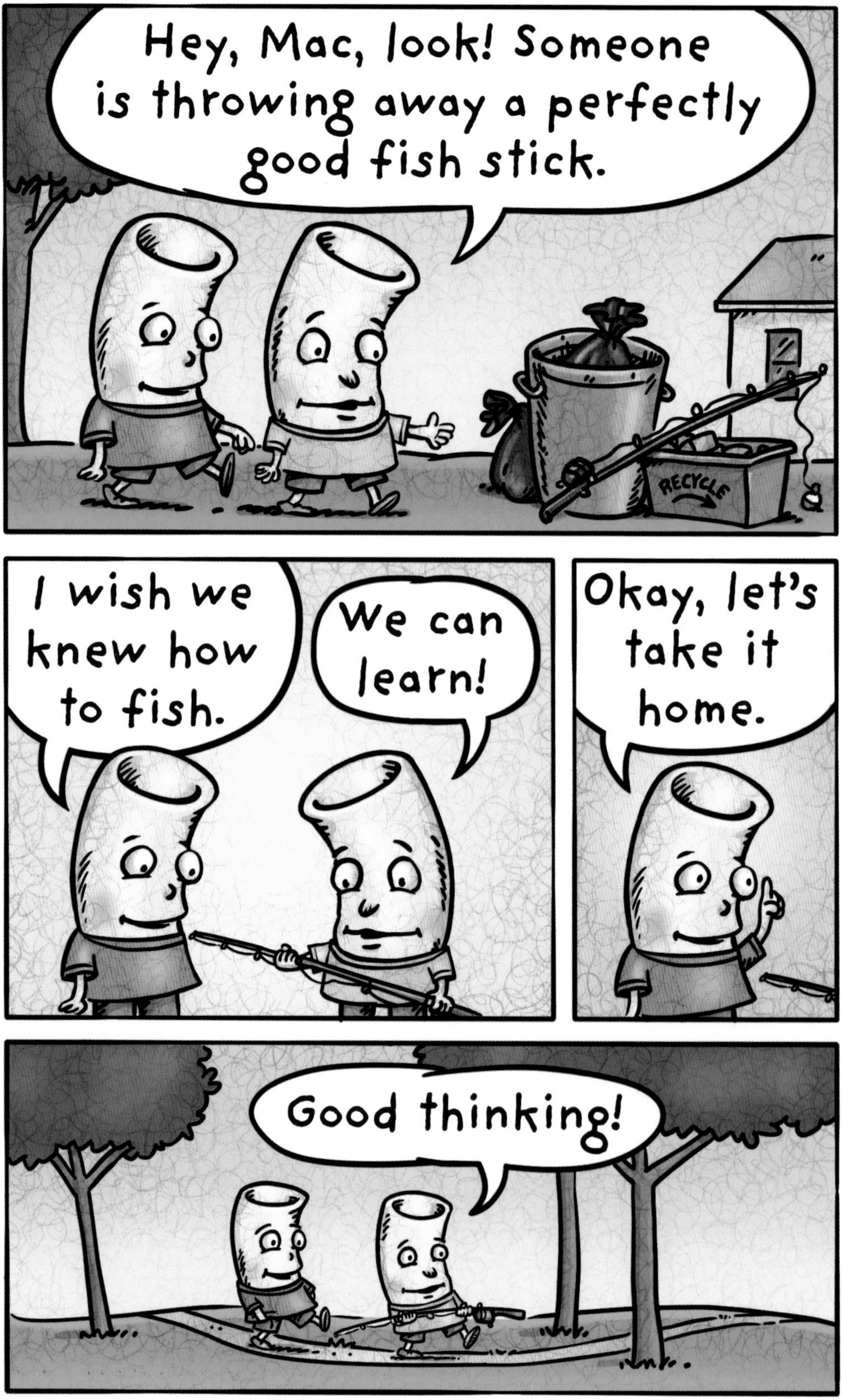
Hey, Mac, look! Someone is throwing away a perfectly good fish stick.
RECYCLE
I wish we knew how to fish.
We can learn!
Okay, let's take it home.
Good thinking!

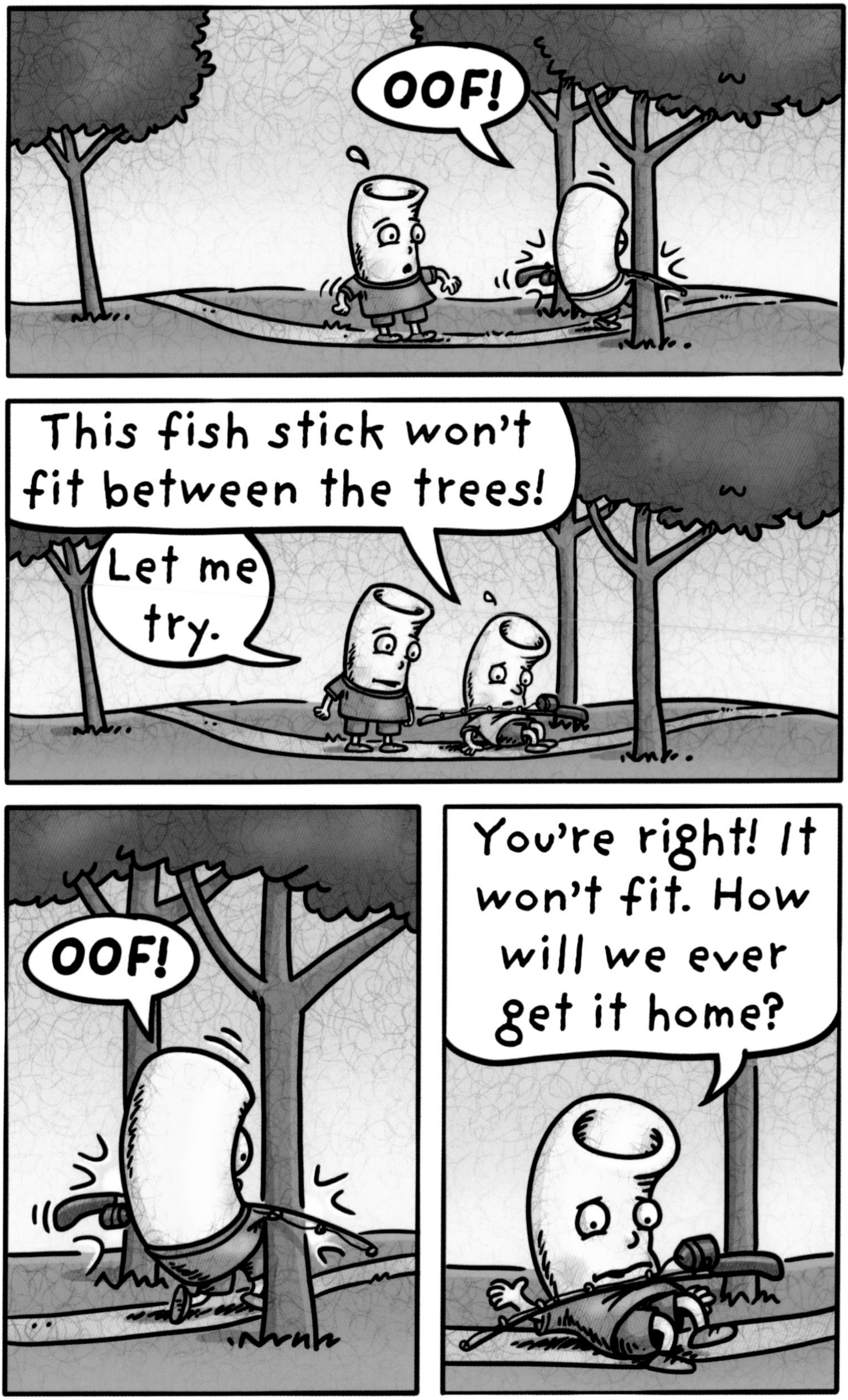
OOF!
This fish stick won't fit between the trees!
Let me try.
OOF!
You're right! It won't fit. How will we ever get it home?

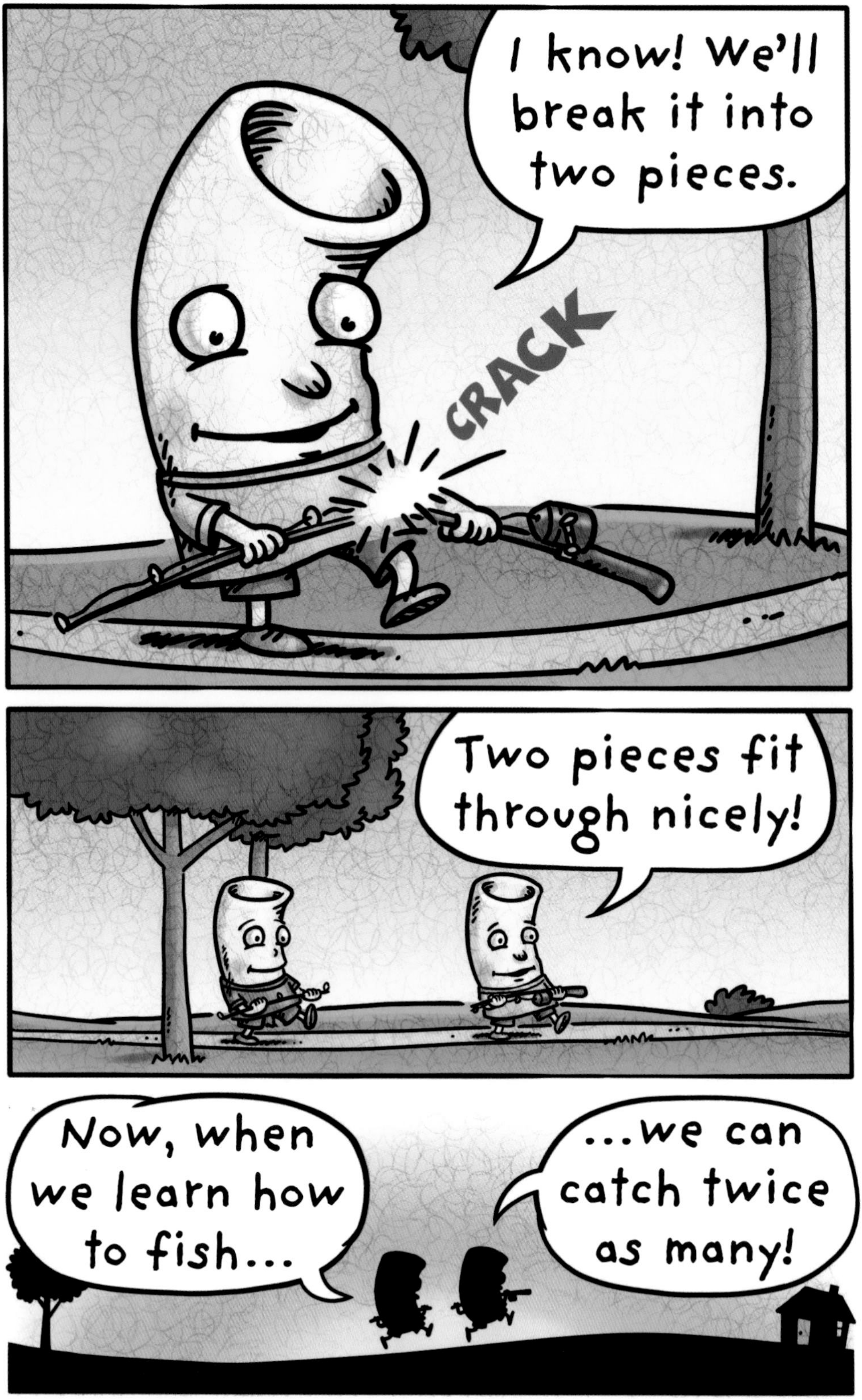
I know! We'll break it into two pieces.
CRACK
Two pieces fit through nicely!
Now, when we learn how to fish...
...we can catch twice as many!

NOODLEHEADS FIND SOMETHING FISHY

CHAPTER 1

HOW TO GROW A BOAT

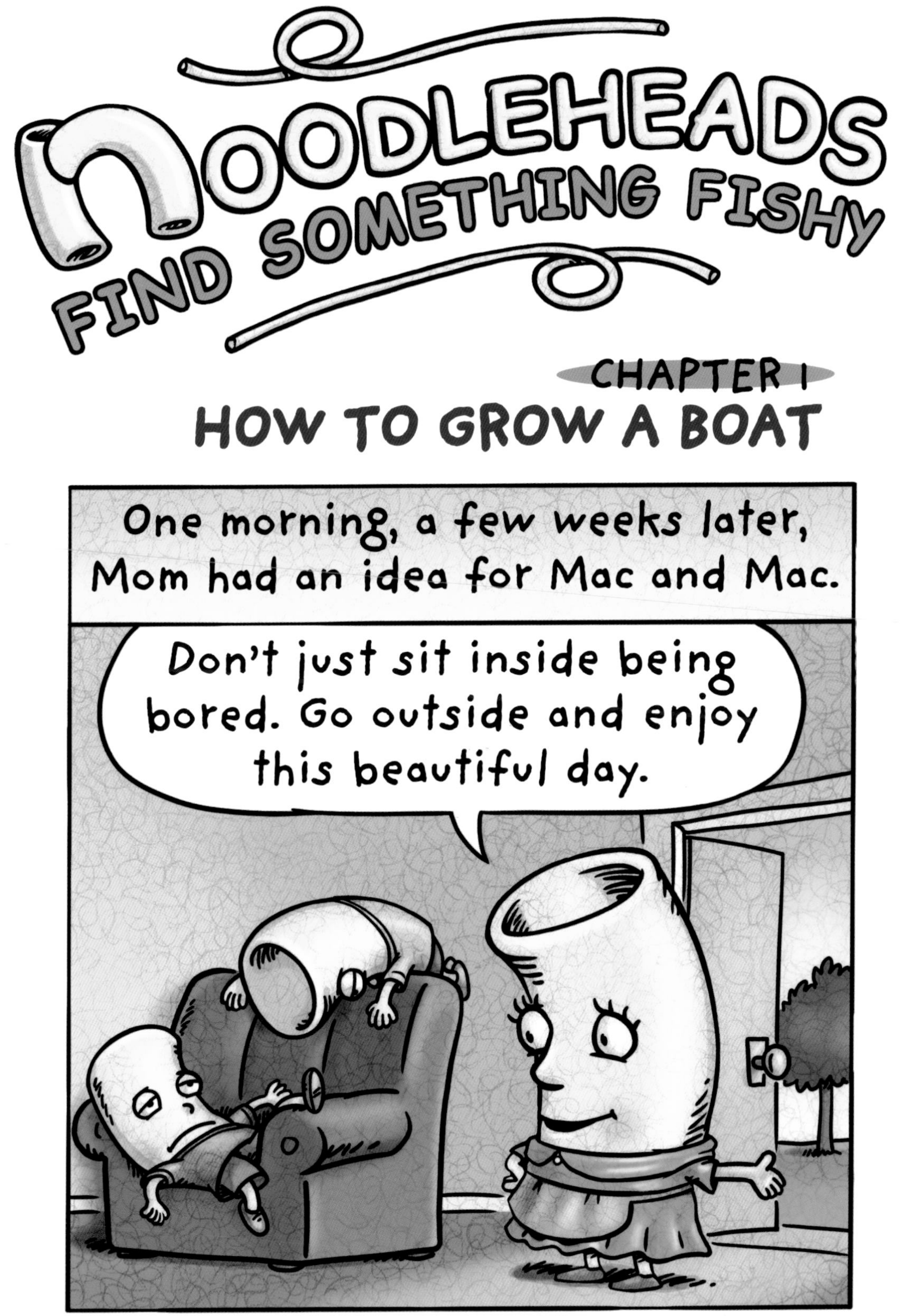
One morning, a few weeks later, Mom had an idea for Mac and Mac.
Don't just sit inside being bored. Go outside and enjoy this beautiful day.

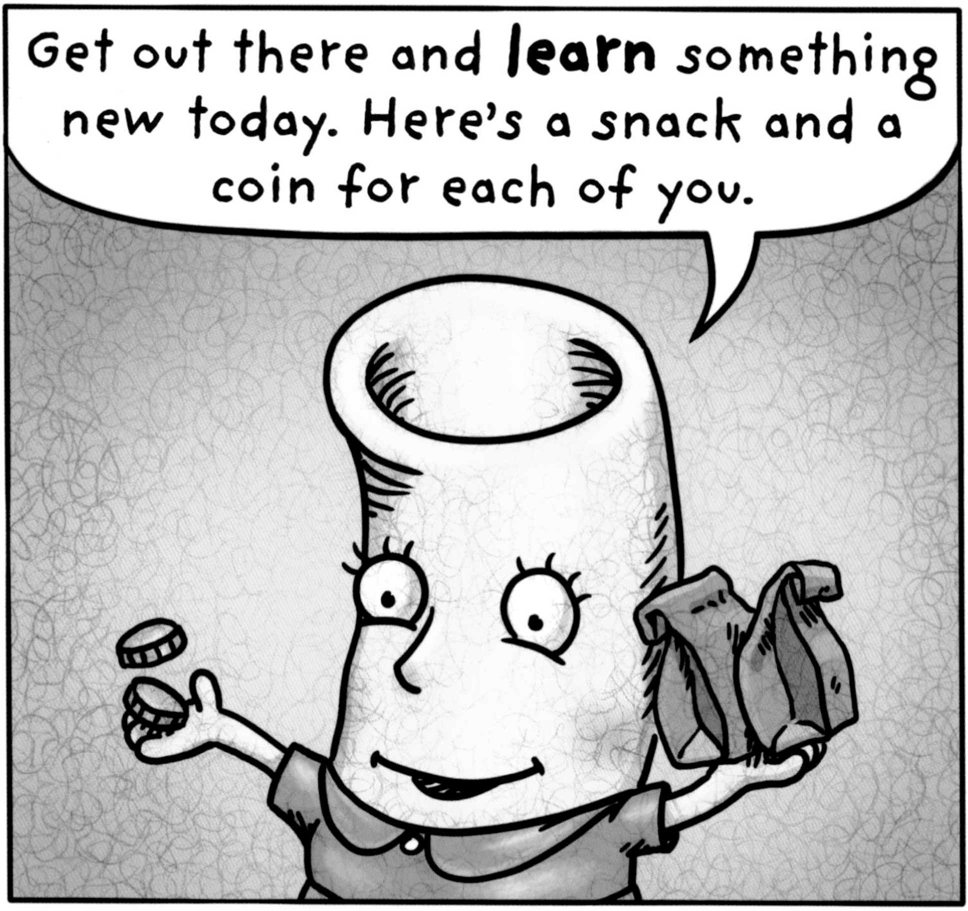
Get out there and **learn** something new today. Here's a snack and a coin for each of you.
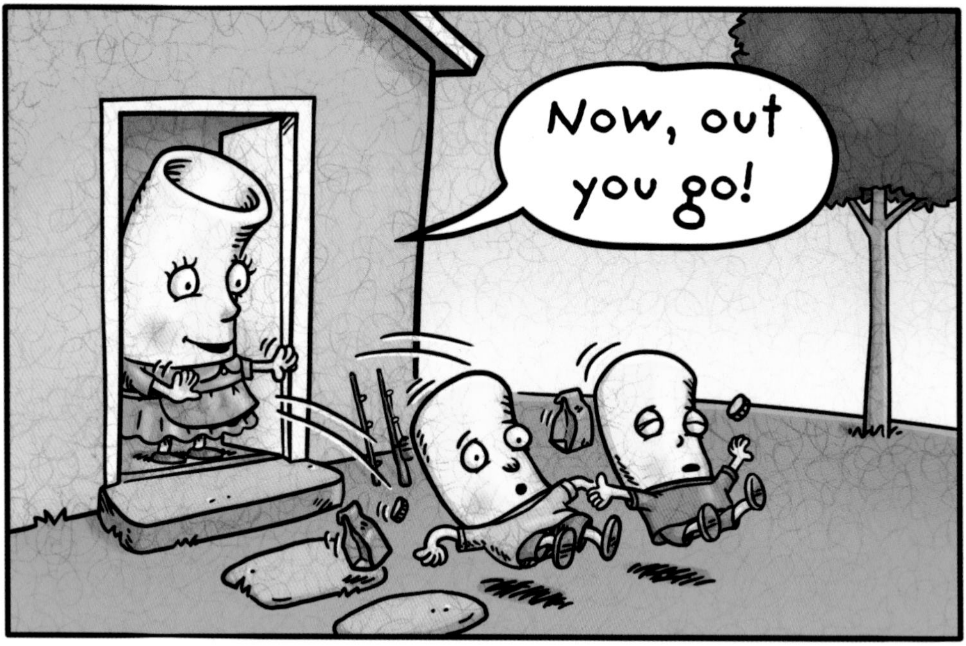
Now, out you go!

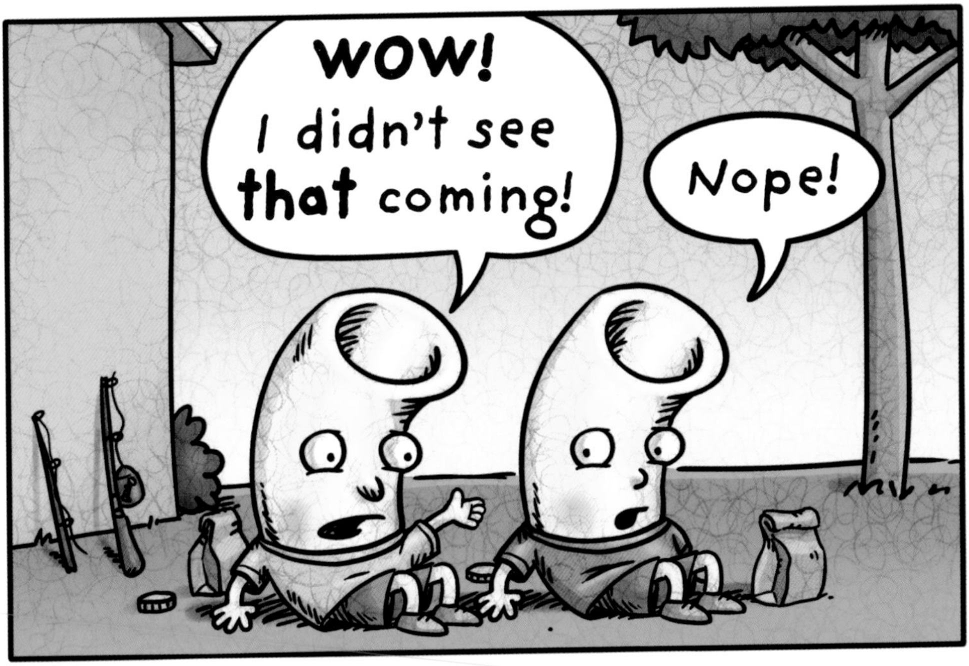
WOW! I didn't see that coming!
Nope!

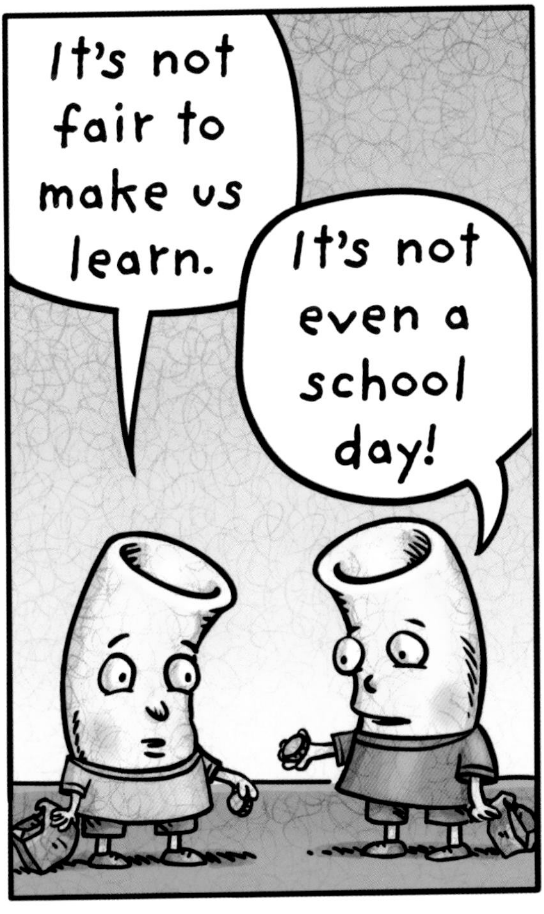
It's not fair to make us learn.
It's not even a school day!

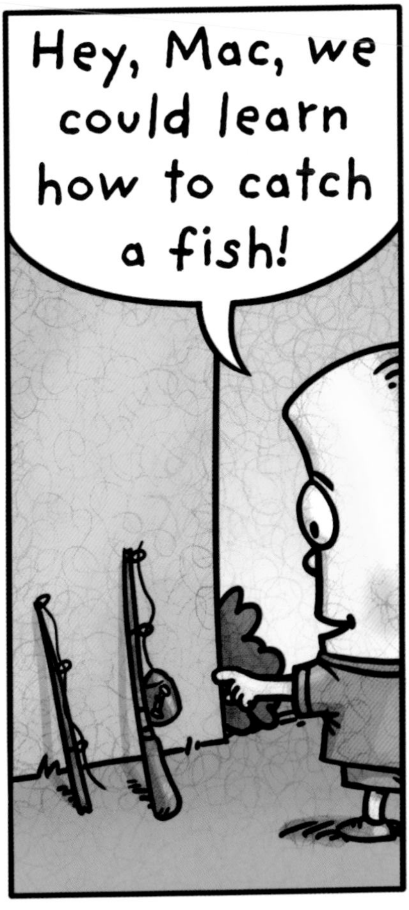
Hey, Mac, we could learn how to catch a fish!

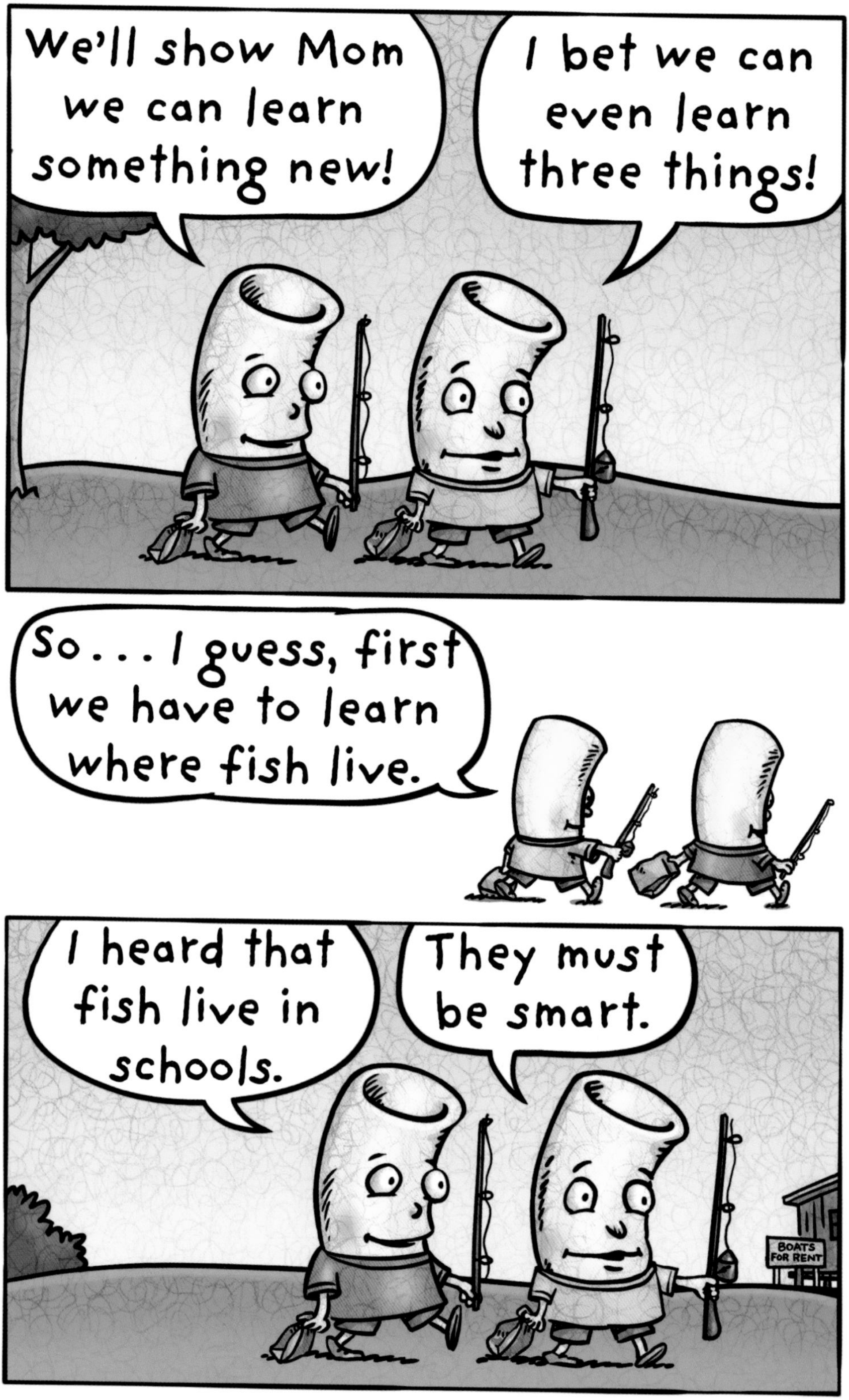
We'll show Mom we can learn something new!
I bet we can even learn three things!
So . . . I guess, first we have to learn where fish live.
I heard that fish live in schools.
They must be smart.
BOATS FOR RENT

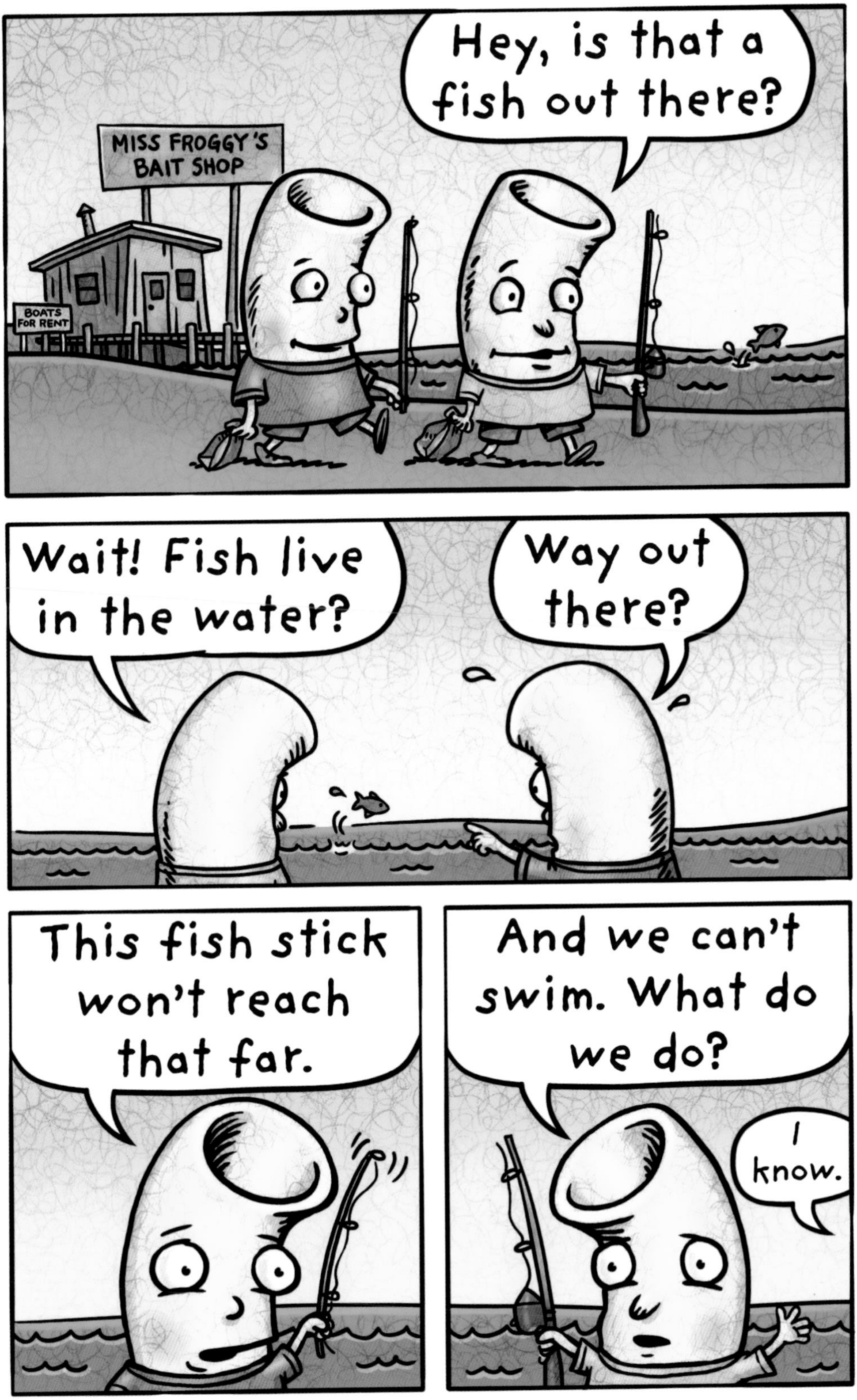
Hey, is that a fish out there?
MISS FROGGY'S BAIT SHOP
BOATS FOR RENT
Wait! Fish live in the water?
Way out there?
This fish stick won't reach that far.
And we can't swim. What do we do?
I know.

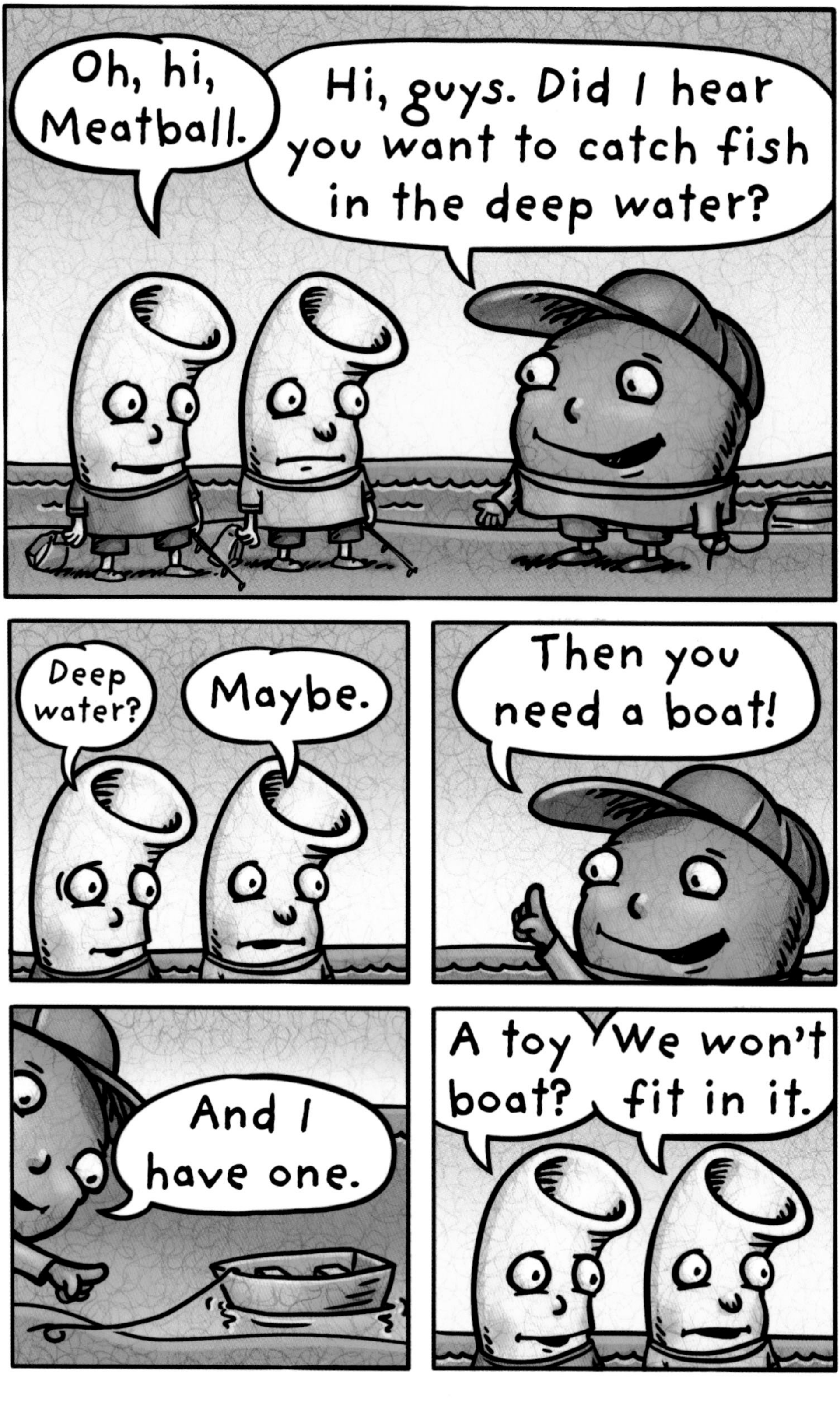

Oh, hi, Meatball.
Hi, guys. Did I hear you want to catch fish in the deep water?
Deep water?
Maybe.
Then you need a boat!
And I have one.
A toy boat?
We won't fit in it.

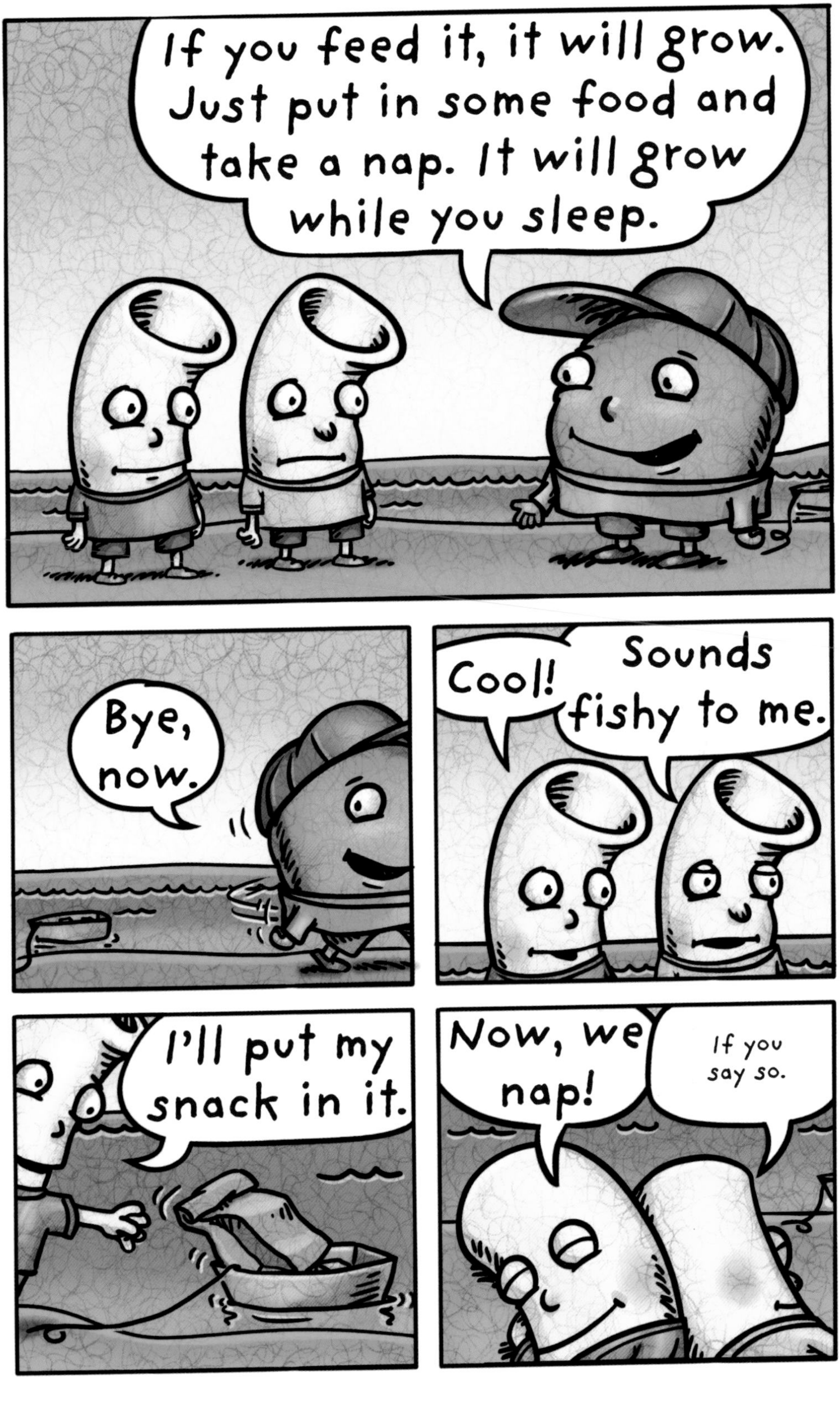
If you feed it, it will grow. Just put in some food and take a nap. It will grow while you sleep.
Bye, now.
Cool!
Sounds fishy to me.
I'll put my snack in it.
Now, we nap!
If you say so.

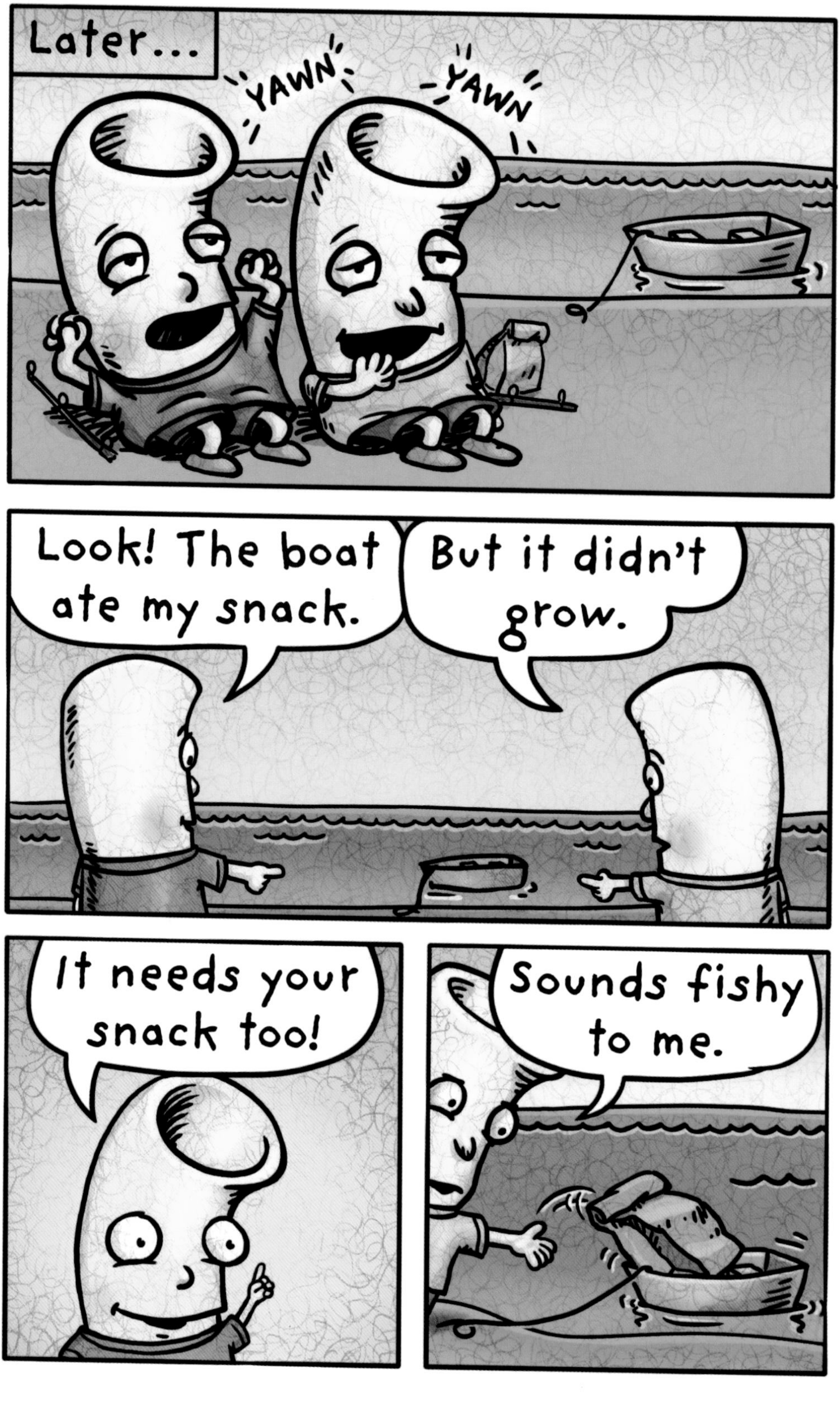
Later...
YAWN
YAWN
Look! The boat ate my snack.
But it didn't grow.
It needs your snack too!
Sounds fishy to me.

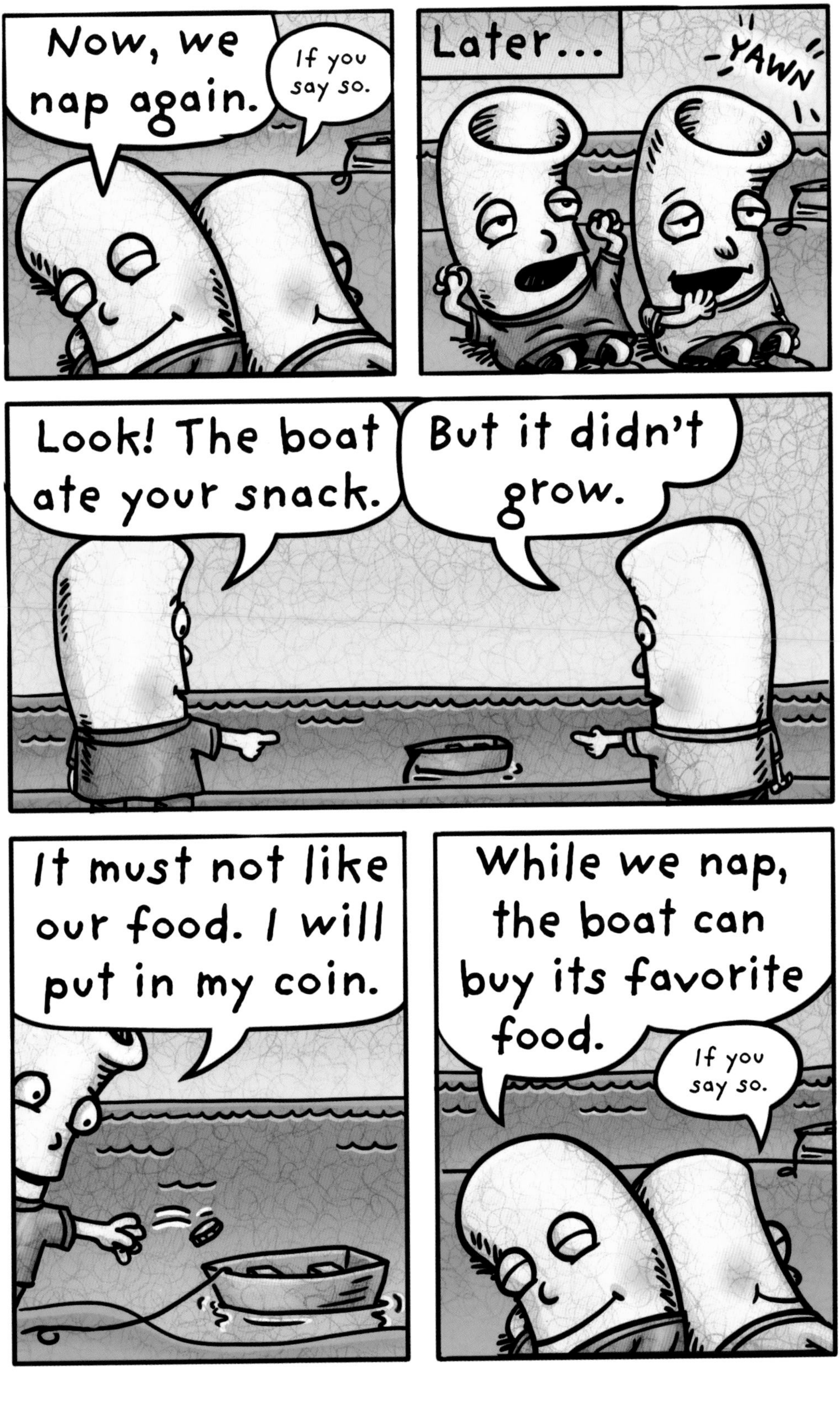
Now, we nap again.
If you say so.
Later...
YAWN
Look! The boat ate your snack.
But it didn't grow.
It must not like our food. I will put in my coin.
While we nap, the boat can buy its favorite food.
If you say so.

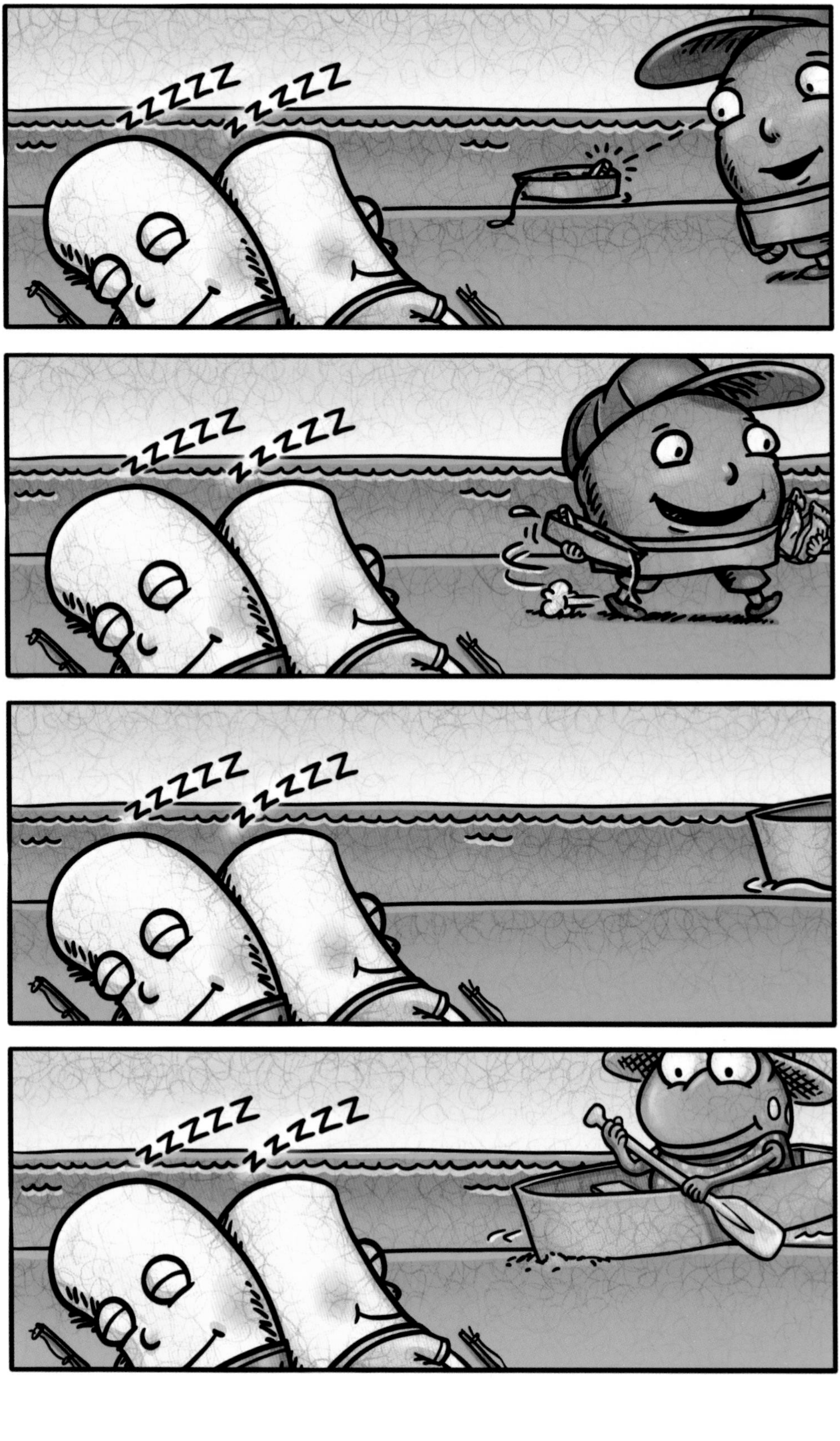
ZZZZZ
ZZZZZ
ZZZZZ
ZZZZZ
ZZZZZ
ZZZZZ
ZZZZZ
ZZZZZ

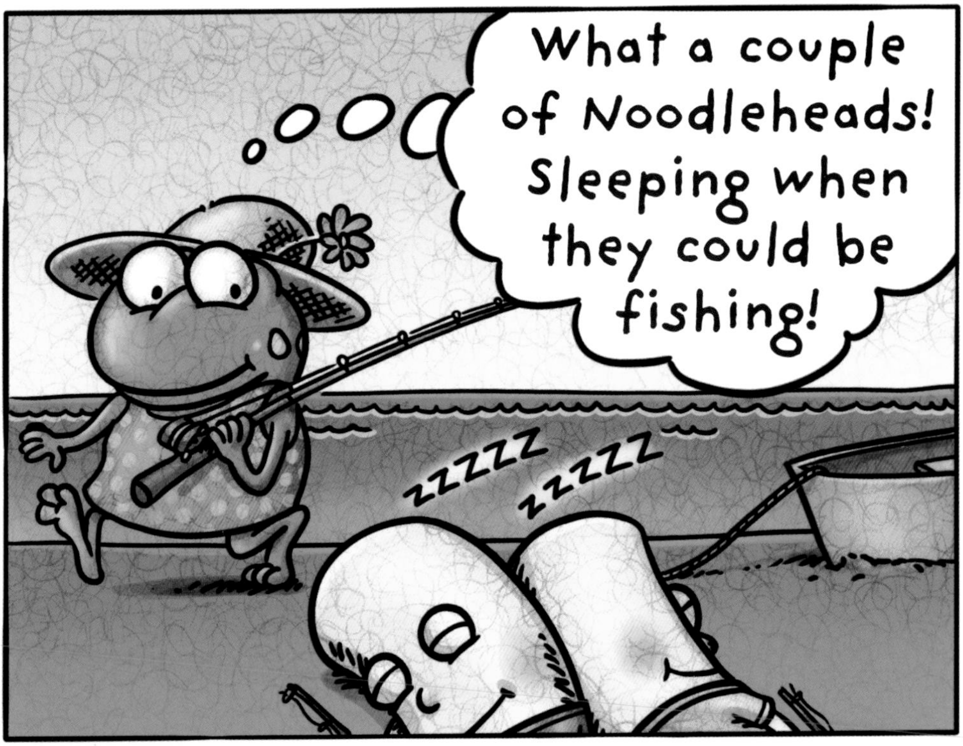
What a couple of Noodleheads! Sleeping when they could be fishing!
ZZZZZ
ZZZZZ

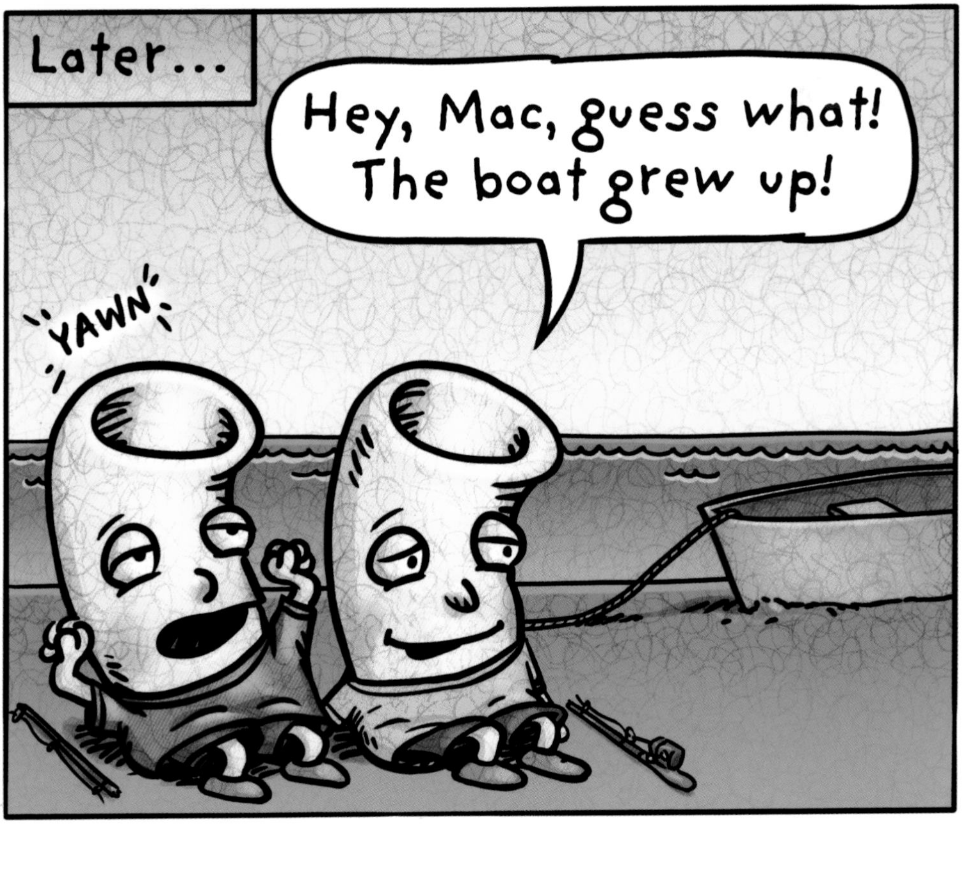
Later...
YAWN
Hey, Mac, guess what! The boat grew up!

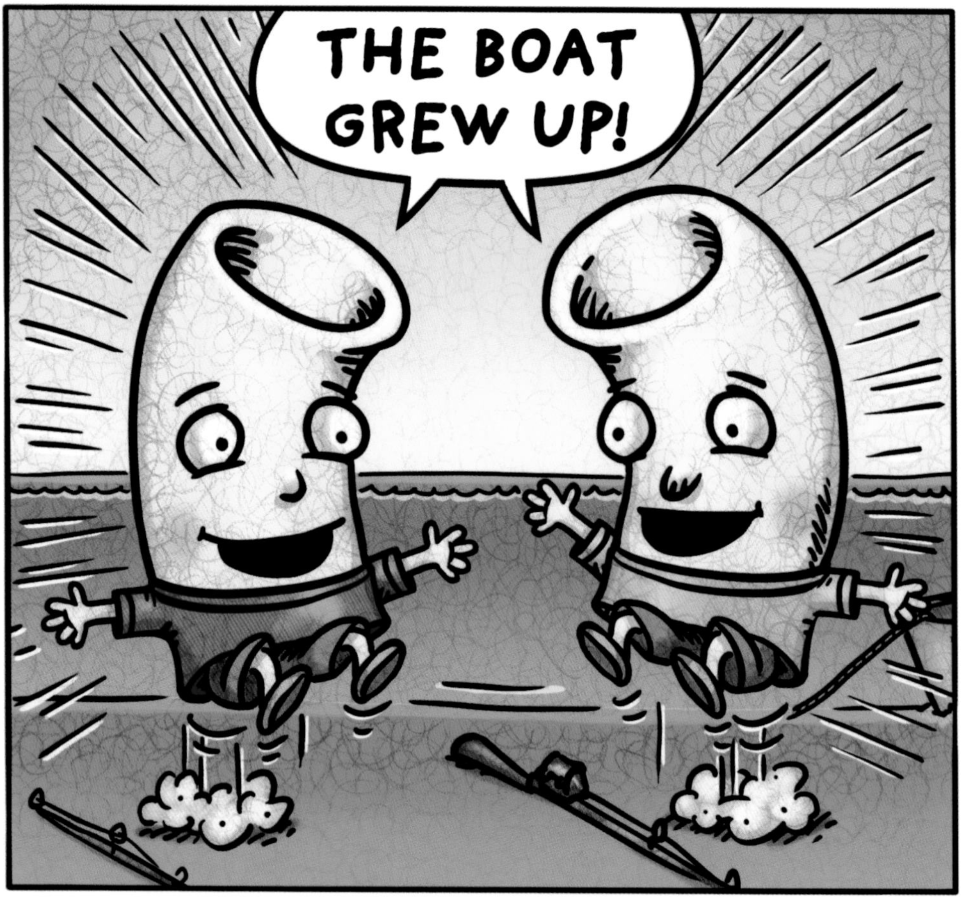
THE BOAT GREW UP!

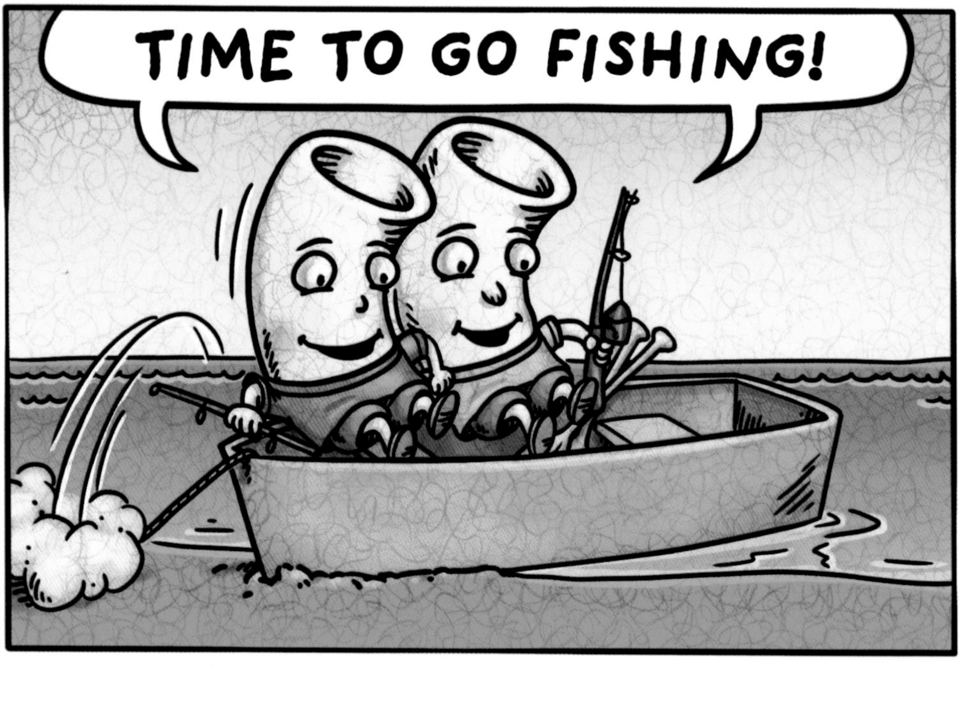
TIME TO GO FISHING!

NOODLEHEADS FIND SOMETHING FISHY

CHAPTER 2
FINDING FISH

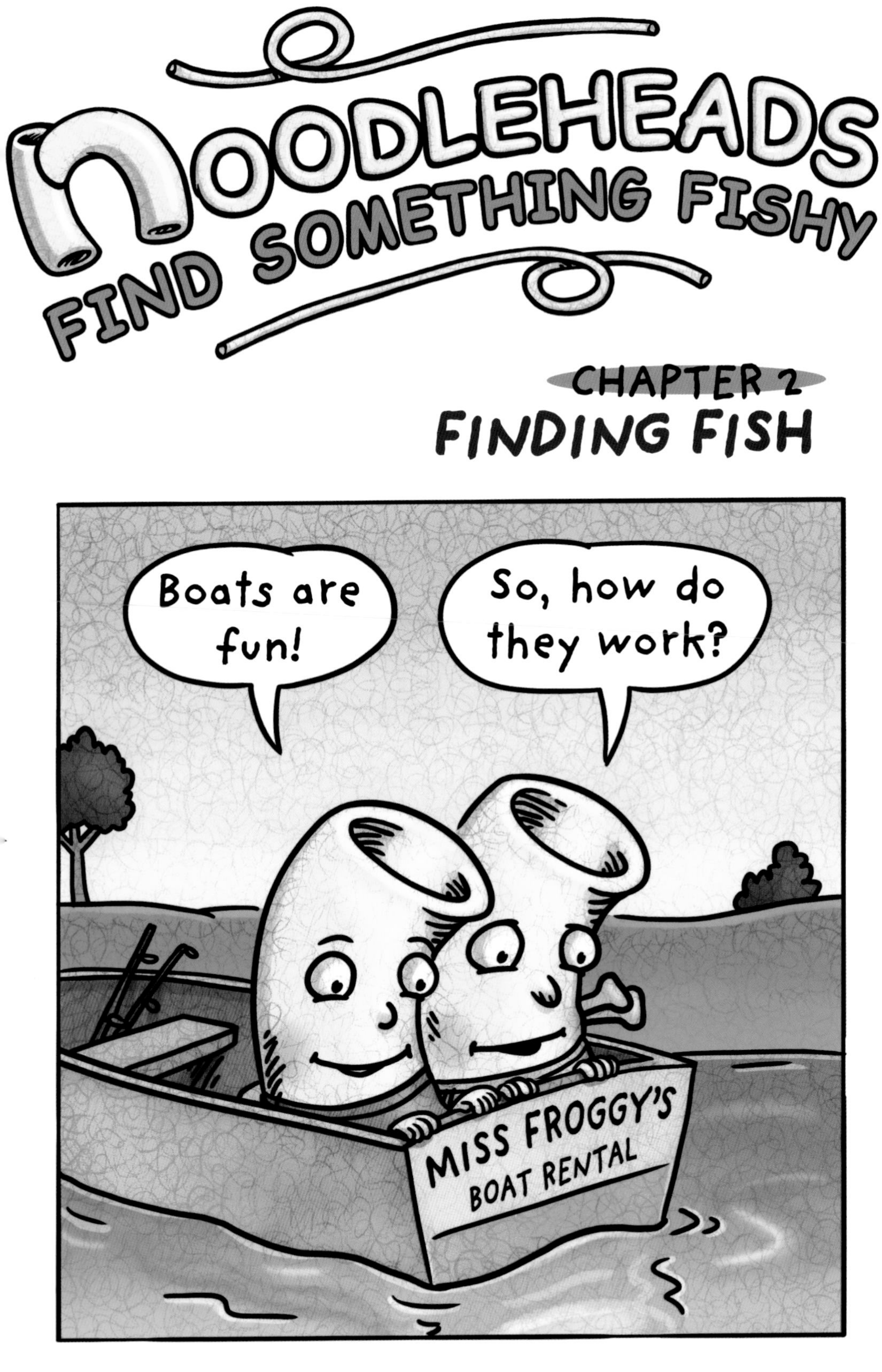
Boats are fun!
So, how do they work?
MISS FROGGY'S BOAT RENTAL

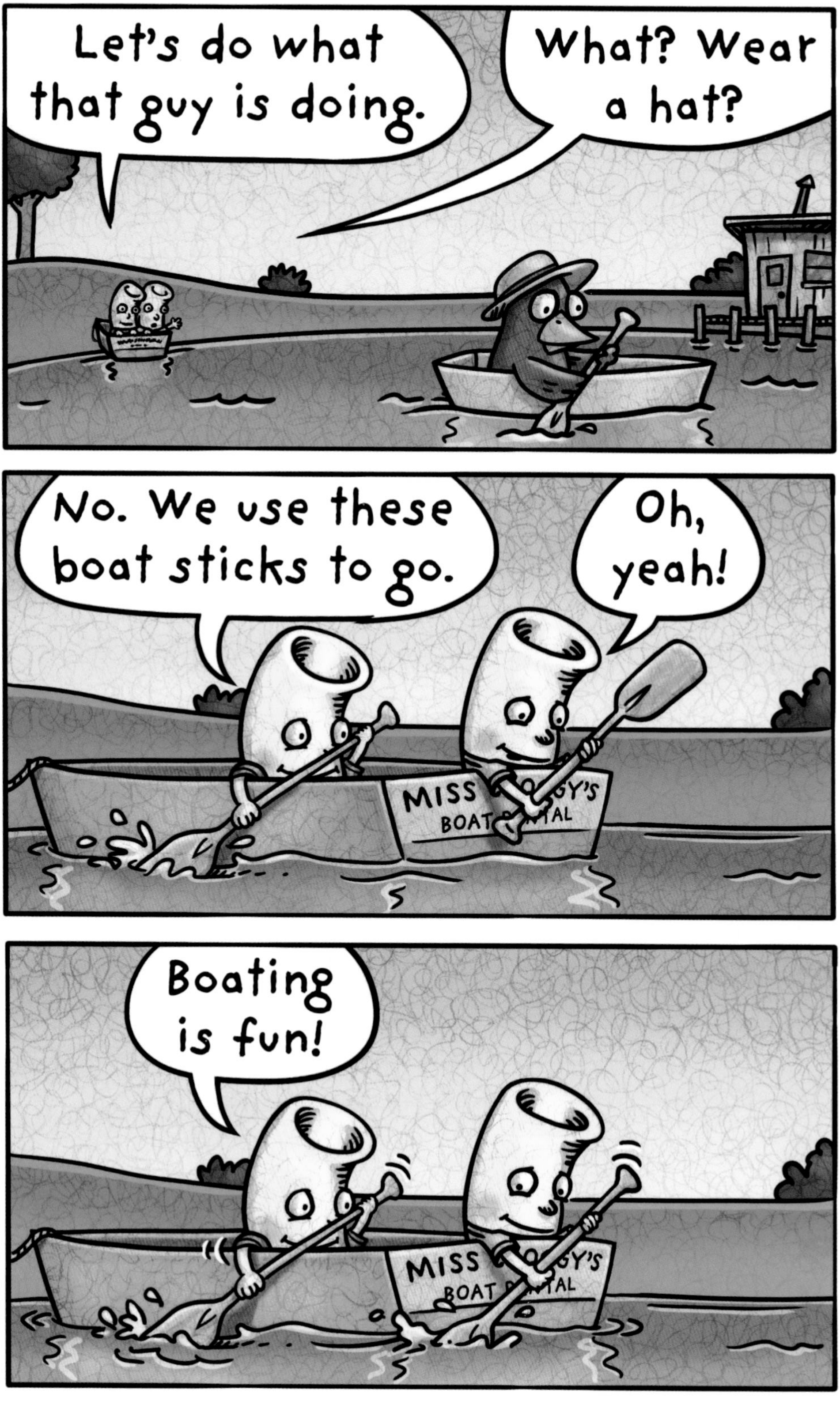
Let's do what that guy is doing.
What? Wear a hat?
No. We use these boat sticks to go.
Oh, yeah!
MISS BOAT
Boating is fun!

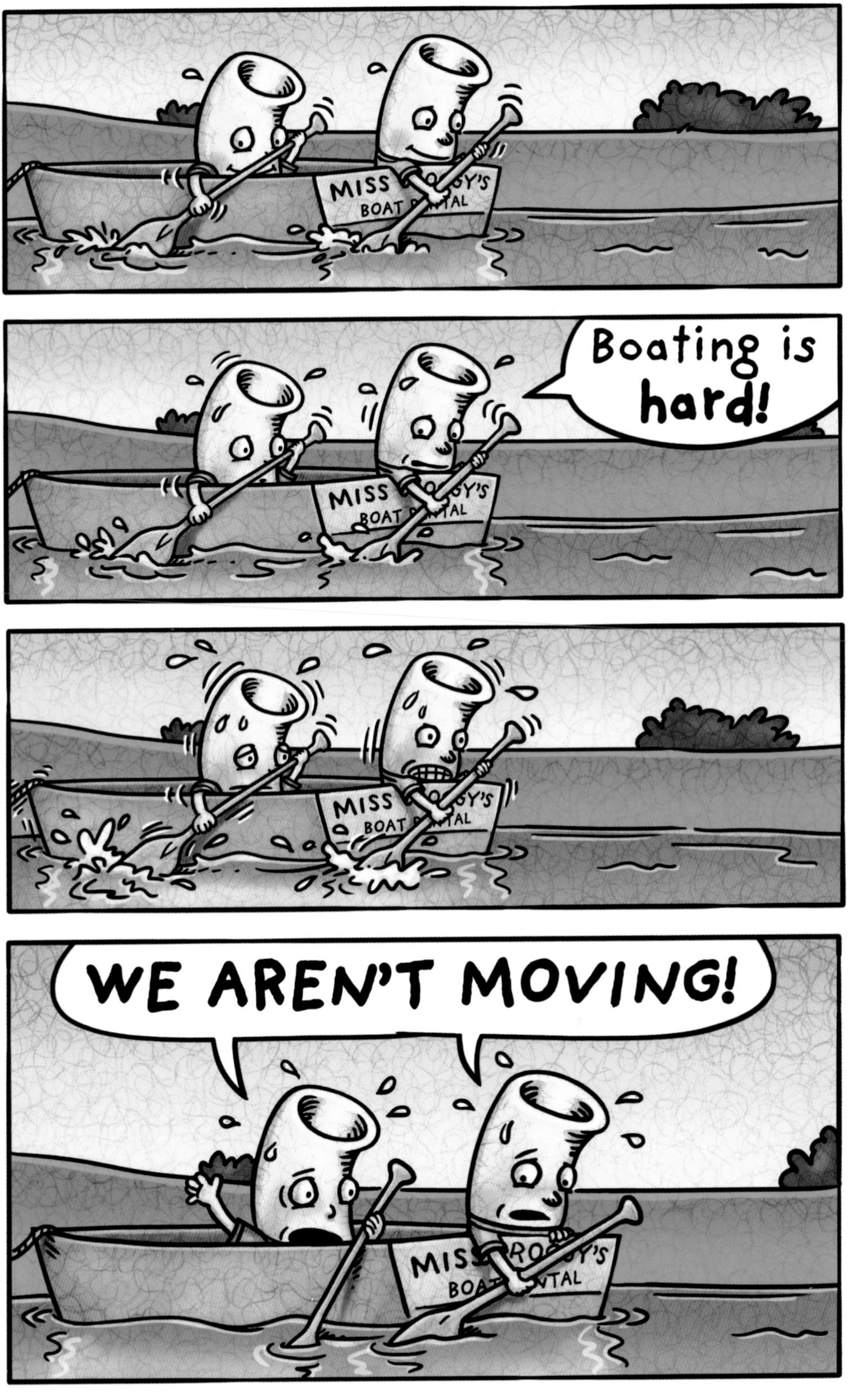
MISS ROSSY'S BOAT RENTAL
Boating is hard!
WE AREN'T MOVING!

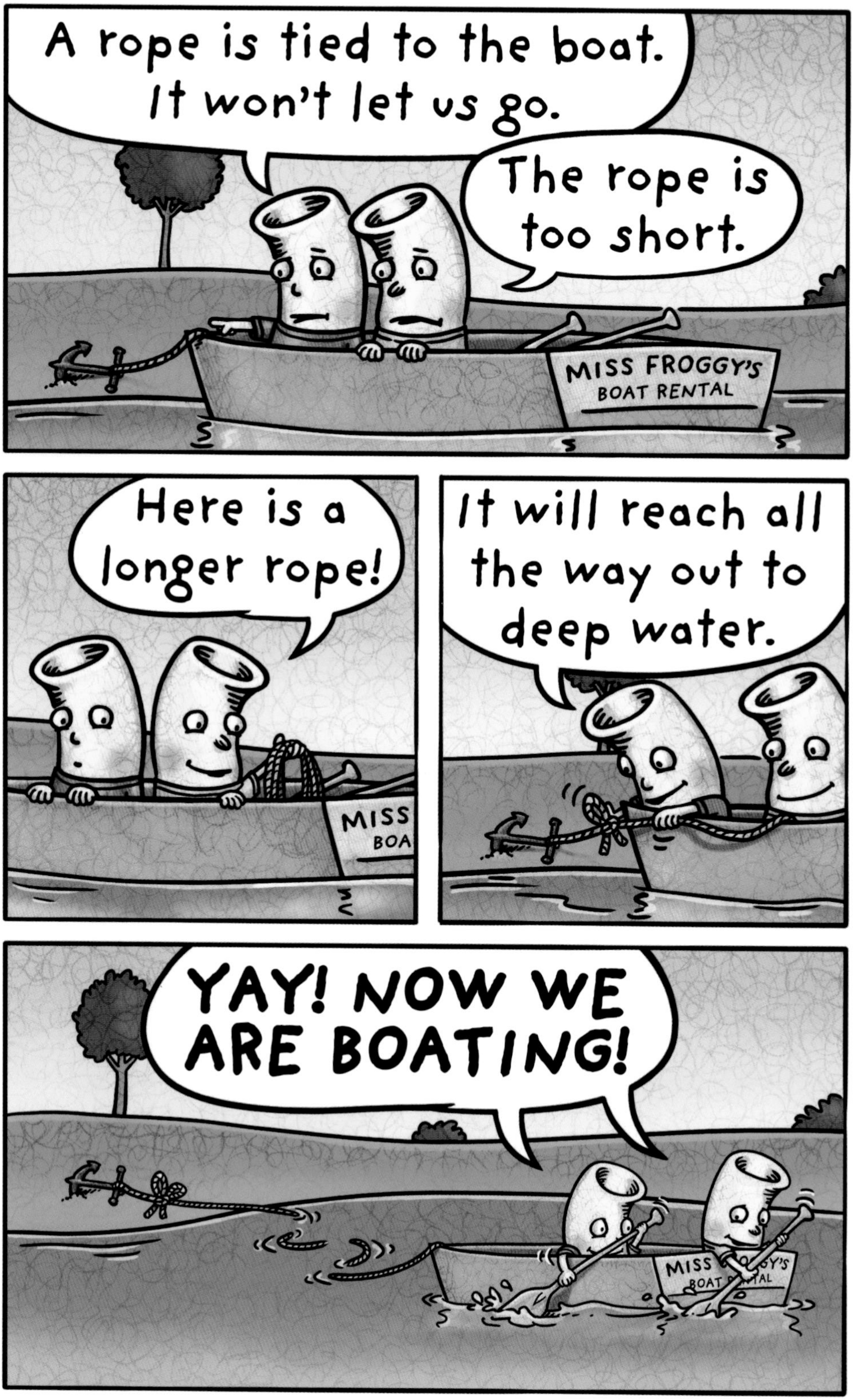
A rope is tied to the boat. It won't let us go.
The rope is too short.
MISS FROGGY'S BOAT RENTAL
Here is a longer rope!
MISS BOA
It will reach all the way out to deep water.
YAY! NOW WE ARE BOATING!

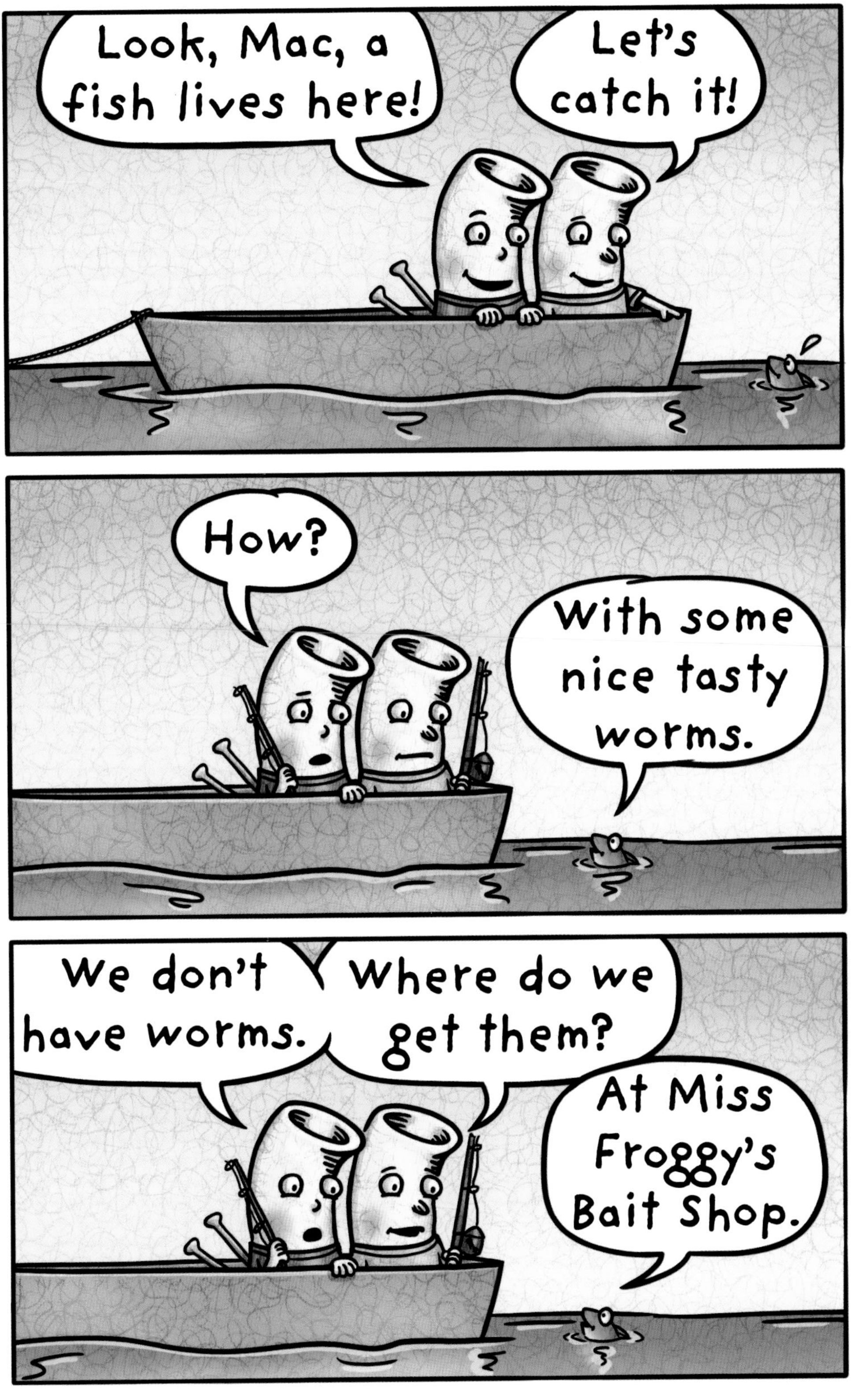
Look, Mac, a fish lives here!
Let's catch it!
How?
With some nice tasty worms.
We don't have worms.
Where do we get them?
At Miss Froggy's Bait Shop.

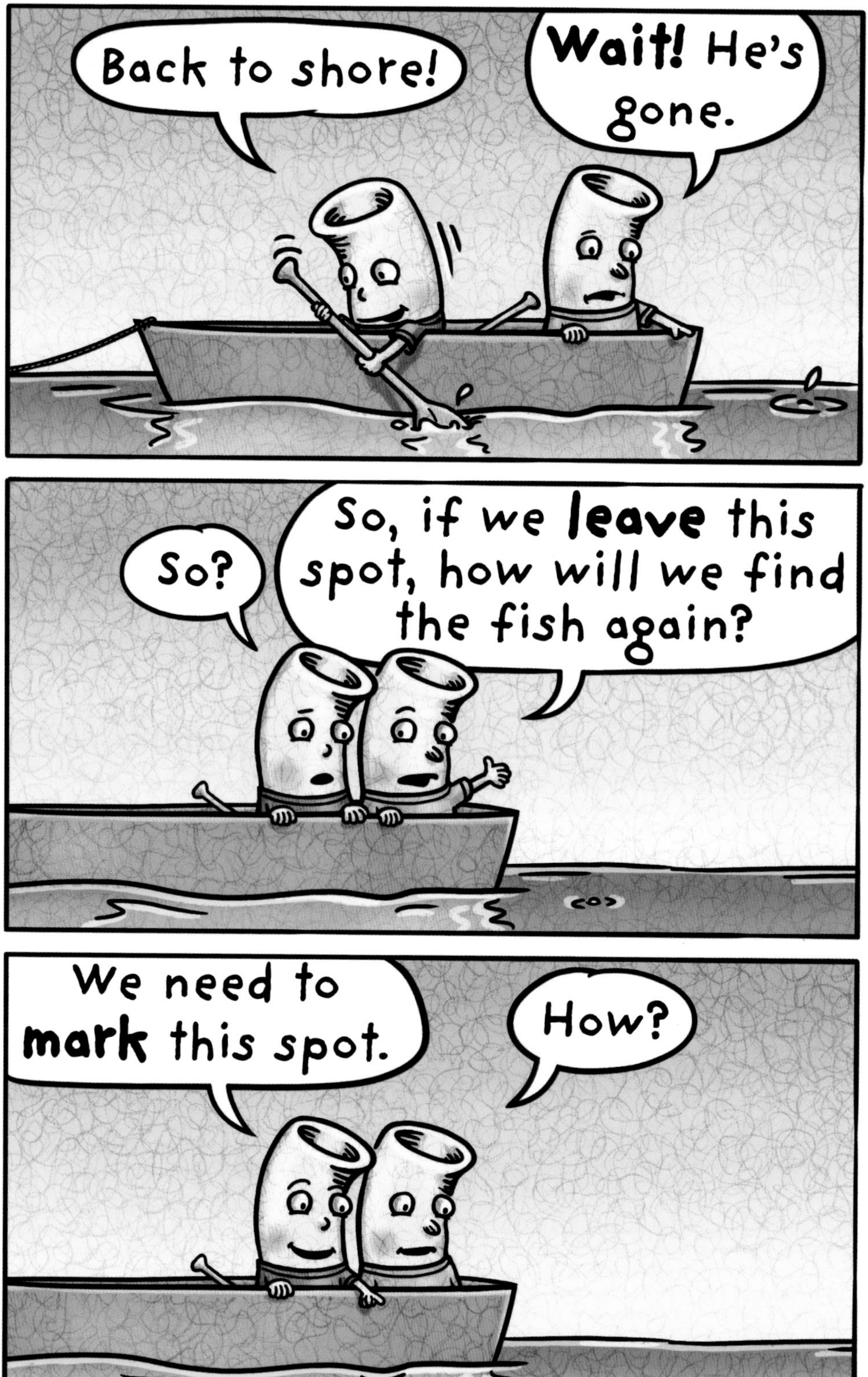

Back to shore!
Wait! He's gone.
So?
So, if we leave this spot, how will we find the fish again?
We need to mark this spot.
How?

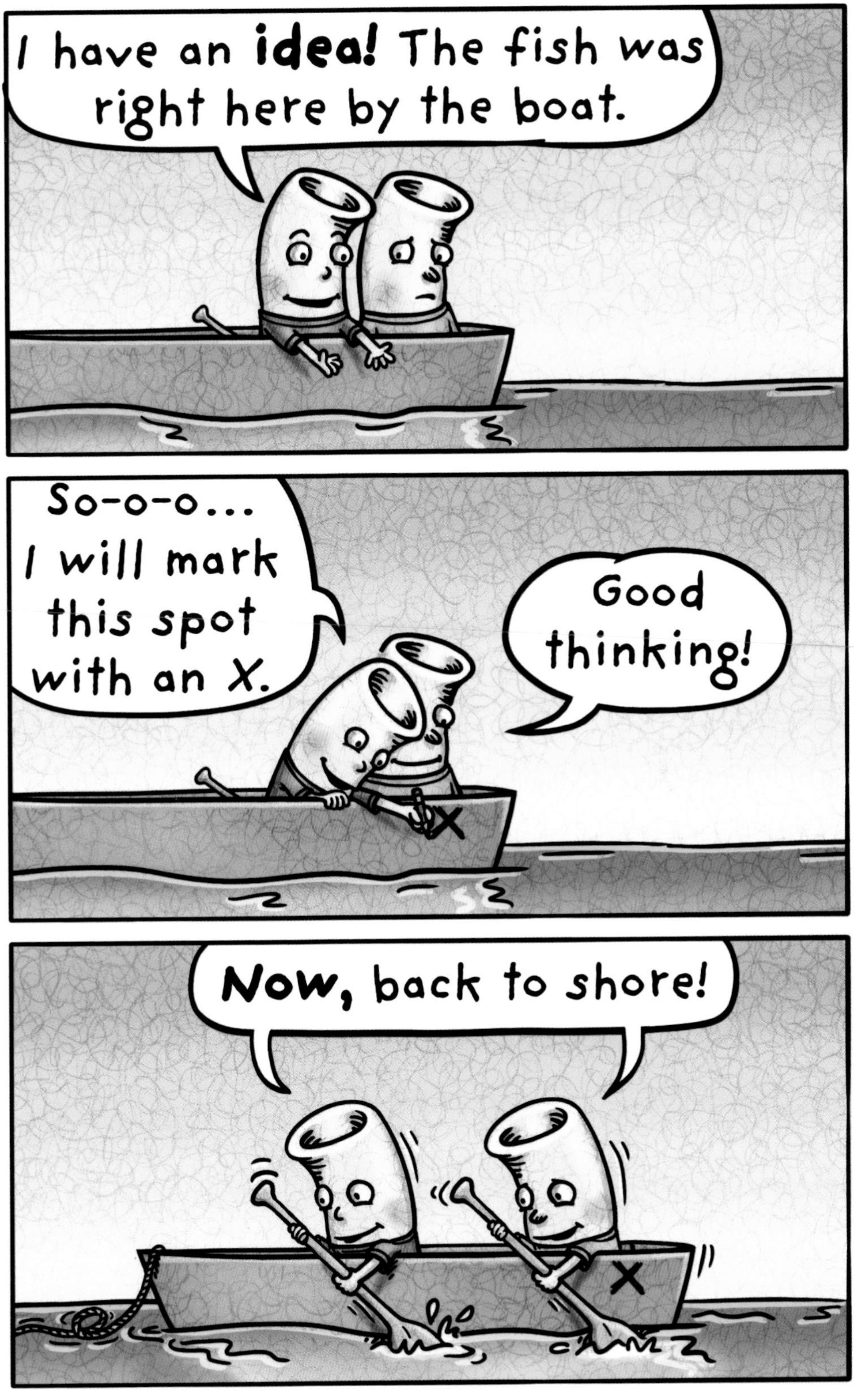
I have an **idea!** The fish was right here by the boat.
So-o-o... I will mark this spot with an X.
Good thinking!
Now, back to shore!

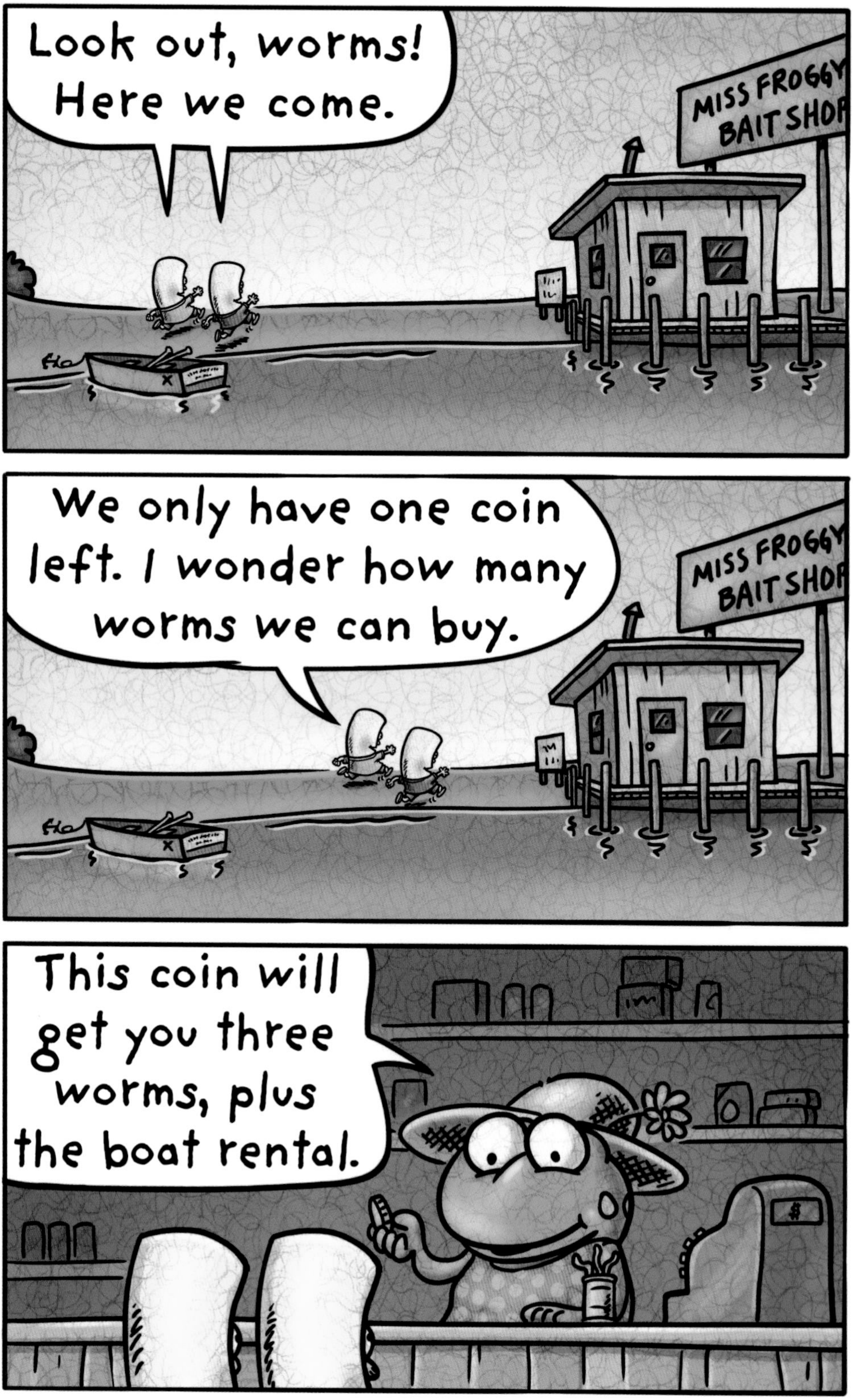
Look out, worms! Here we come.
We only have one coin left. I wonder how many worms we can buy.
This coin will get you three worms, plus the boat rental.

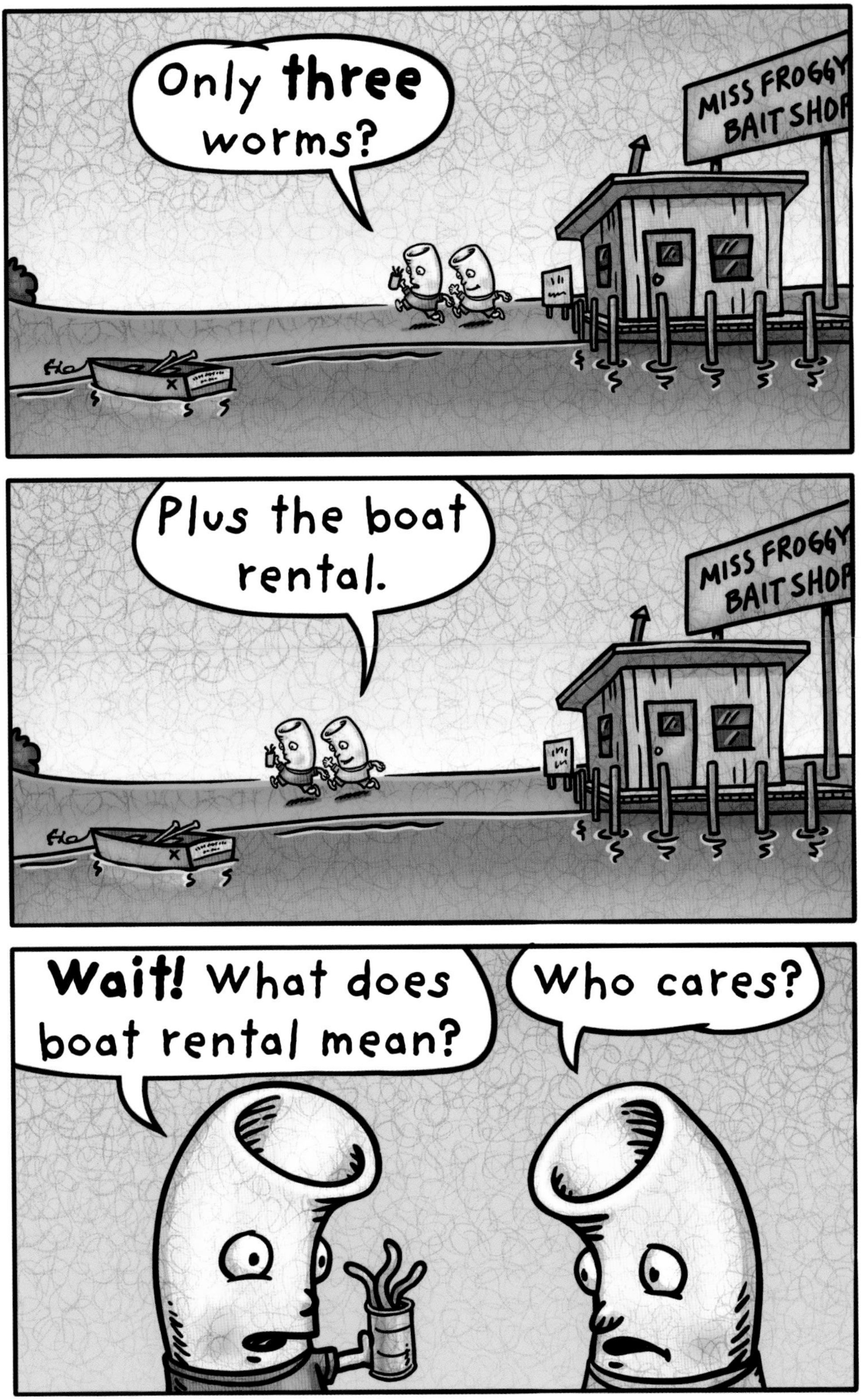
Only three worms?
MISS FROGGY BAIT SHOP
Plus the boat rental.
MISS FROGGY BAIT SHOP
Wait! What does boat rental mean?
Who cares?

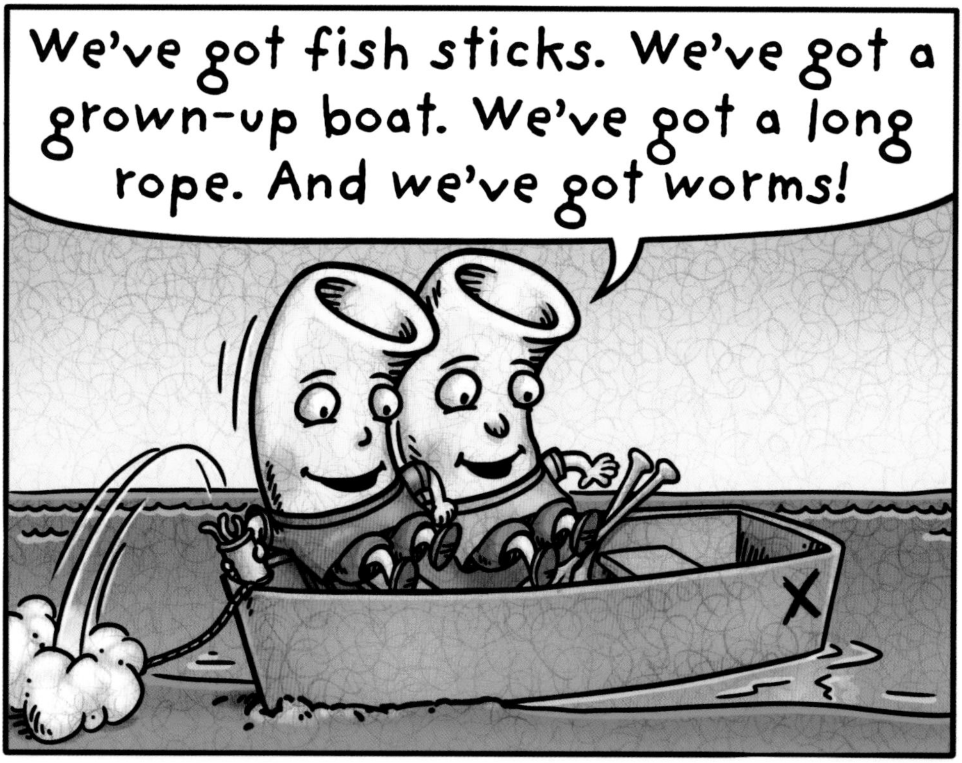
We've got fish sticks. We've got a grown-up boat. We've got a long rope. And we've got worms!

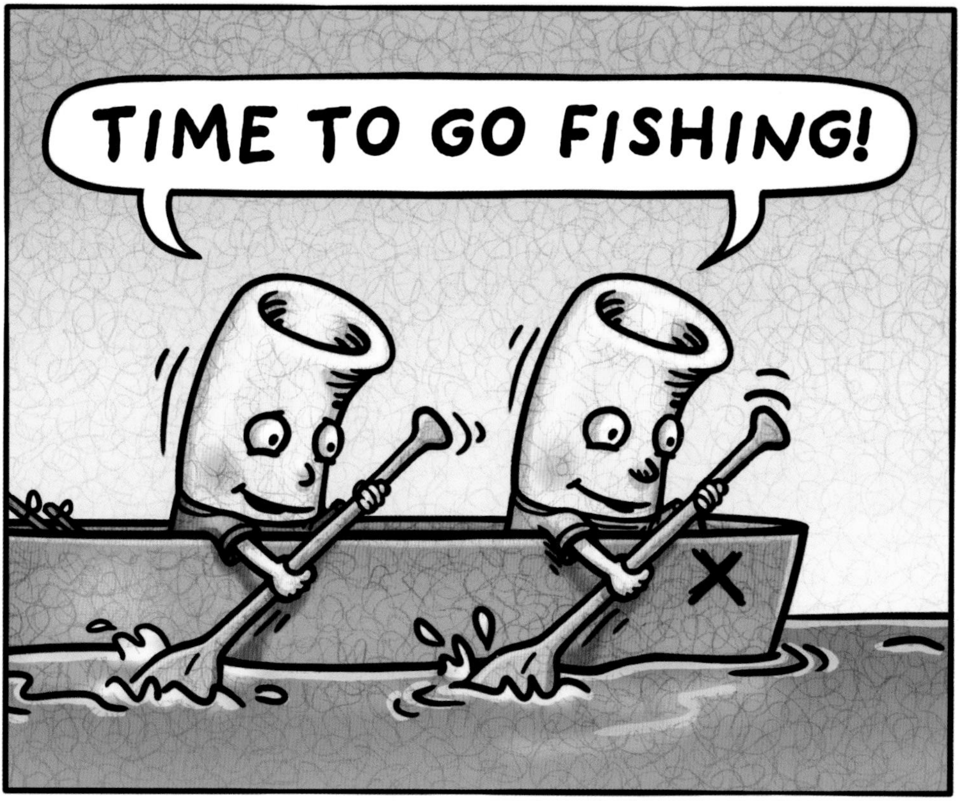
TIME TO GO FISHING!

NOODLEHEADS FIND SOMETHING FISHY

CHAPTER 3
THE BIGGEST FISH

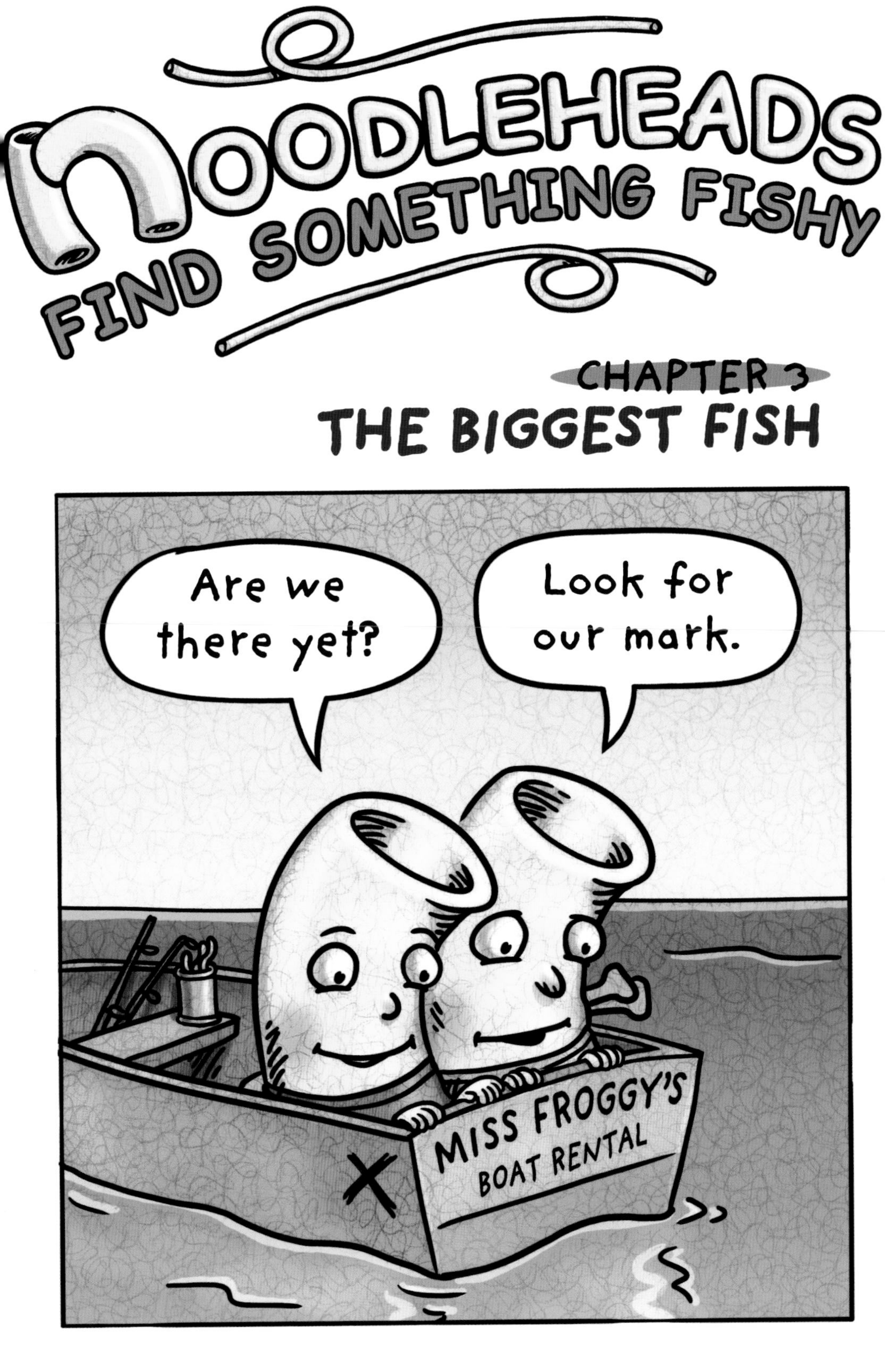
Are we there yet?
Look for our mark.
MISS FROGGY'S BOAT RENTAL

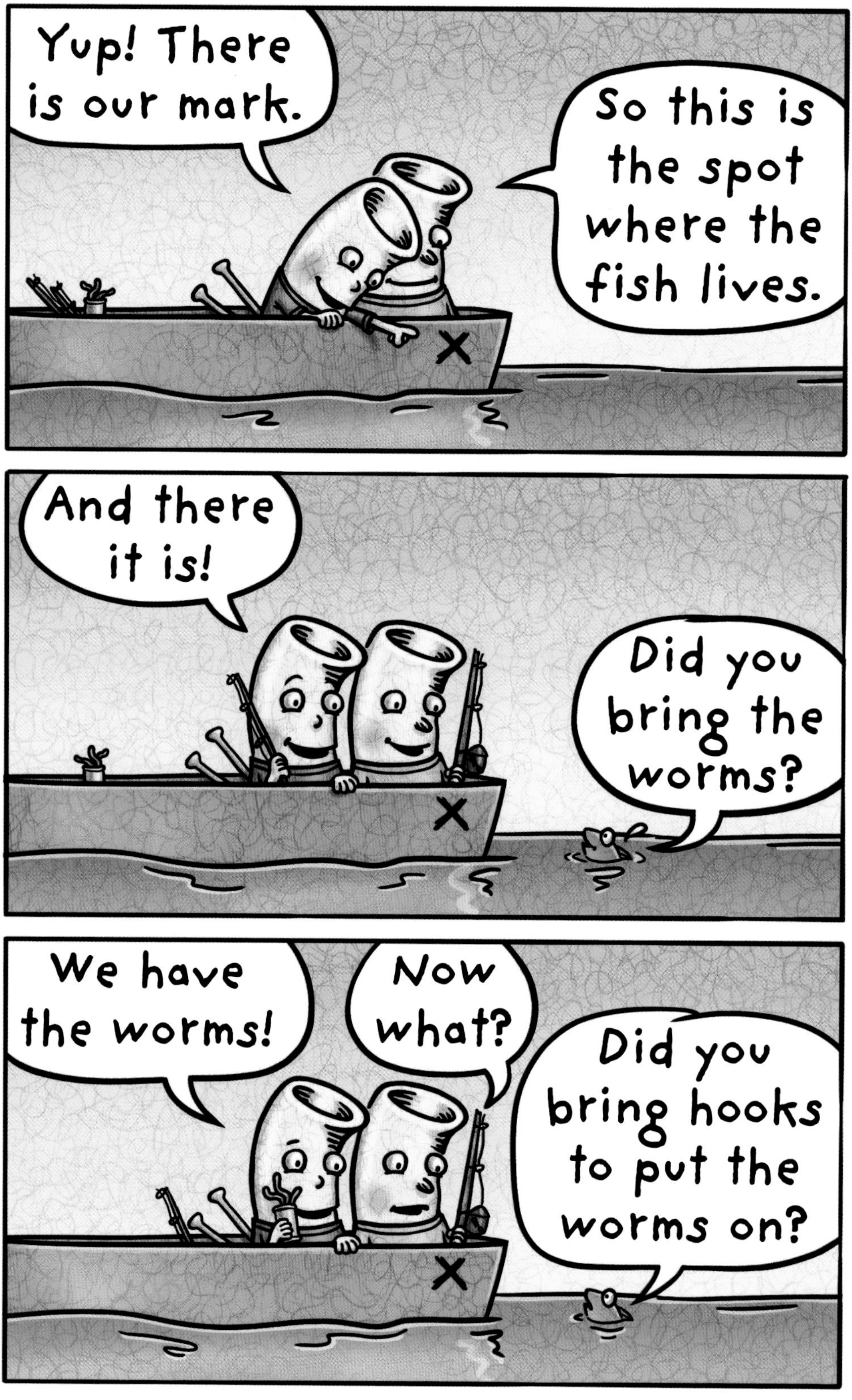
Yup! There is our mark.
So this is the spot where the fish lives.
And there it is!
Did you bring the worms?
We have the worms!
Now what?
Did you bring hooks to put the worms on?

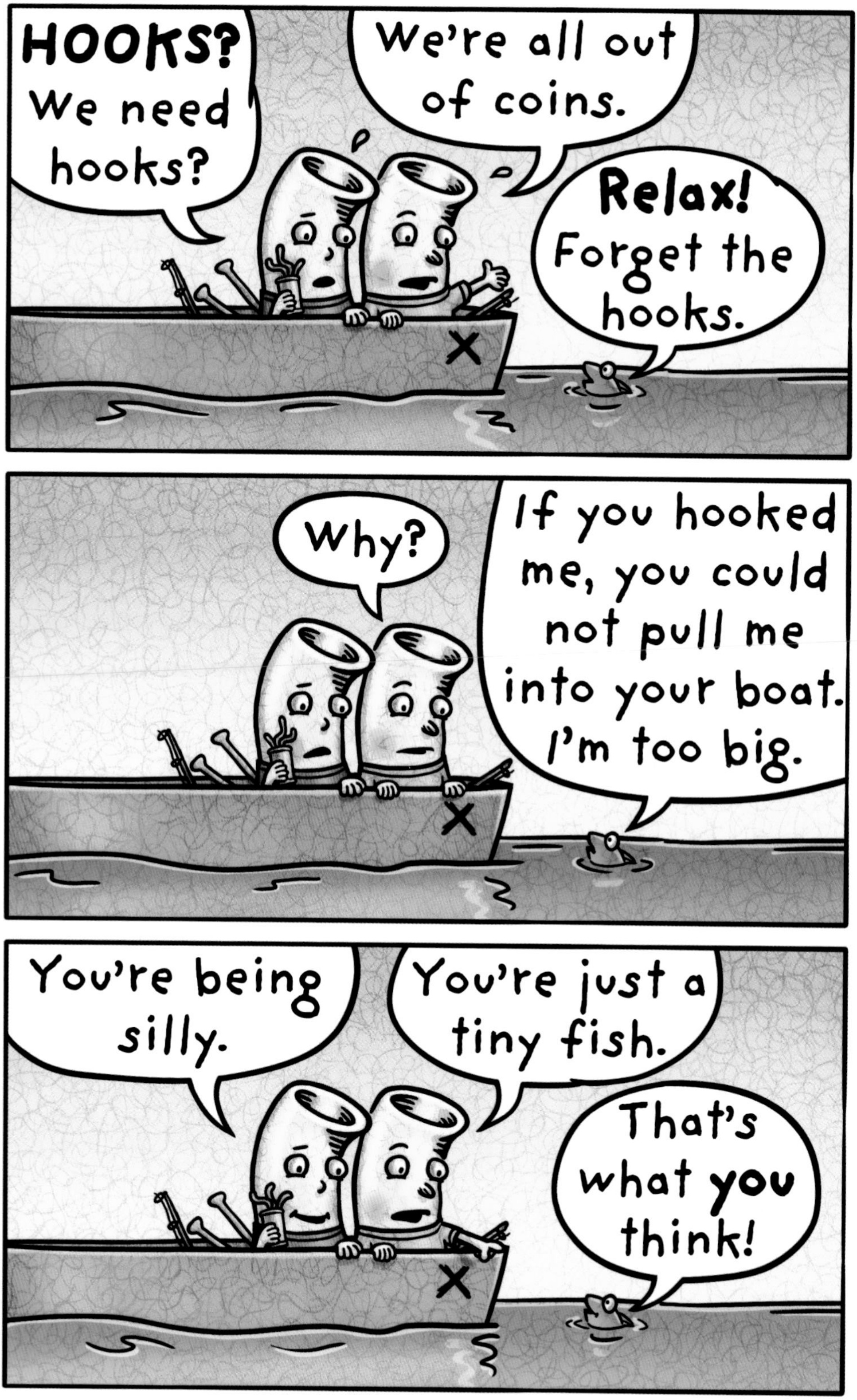
HOOKS? We need hooks?
We're all out of coins.
Relax! Forget the hooks.
Why?
If you hooked me, you could not pull me into your boat. I'm too big.
You're being silly.
You're just a tiny fish.
That's what you think!

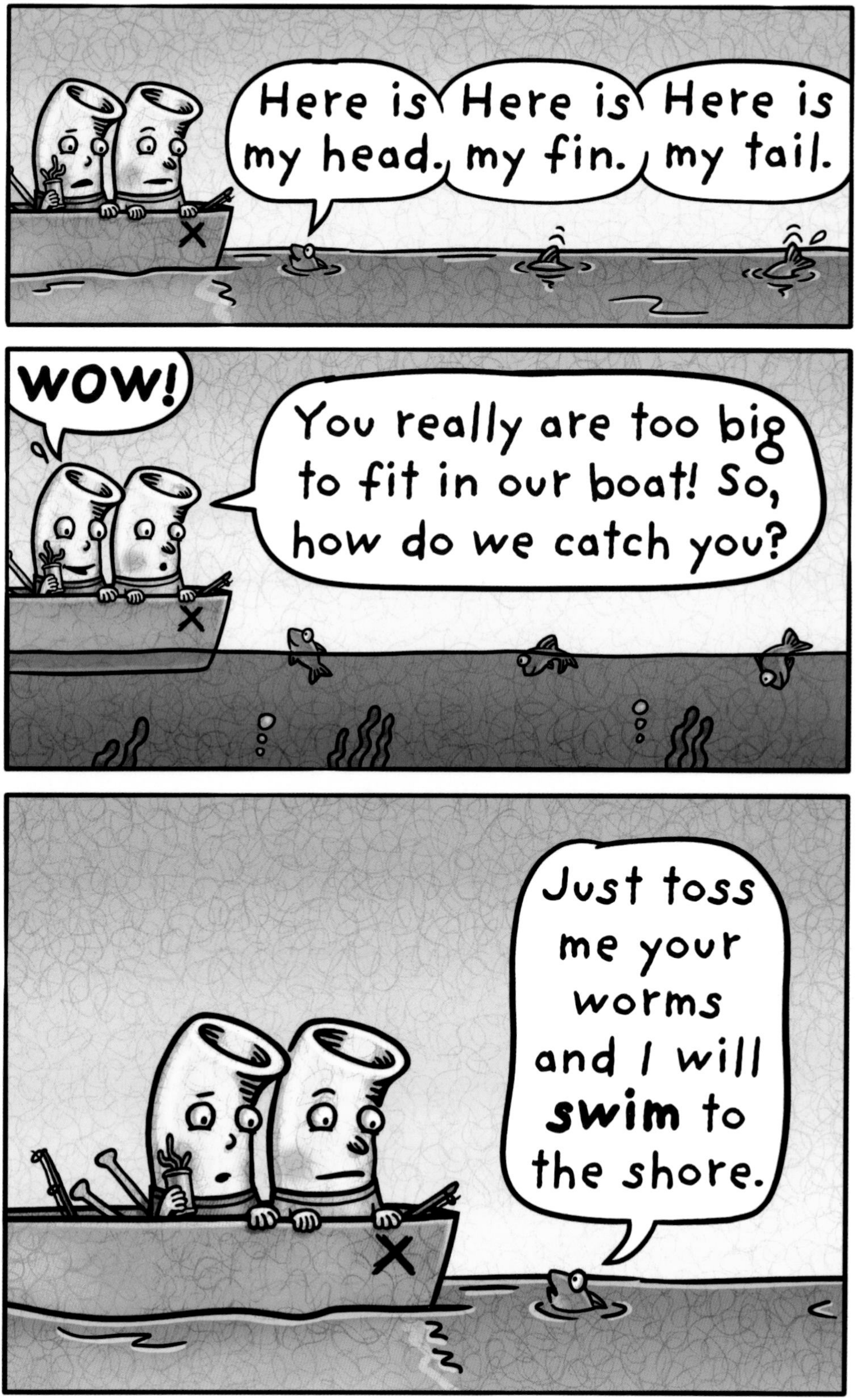
Here is my head.
Here is my fin.
Here is my tail.
WOW!
You really are too big to fit in our boat! So, how do we catch you?
Just toss me your worms and I will **swim** to the shore.

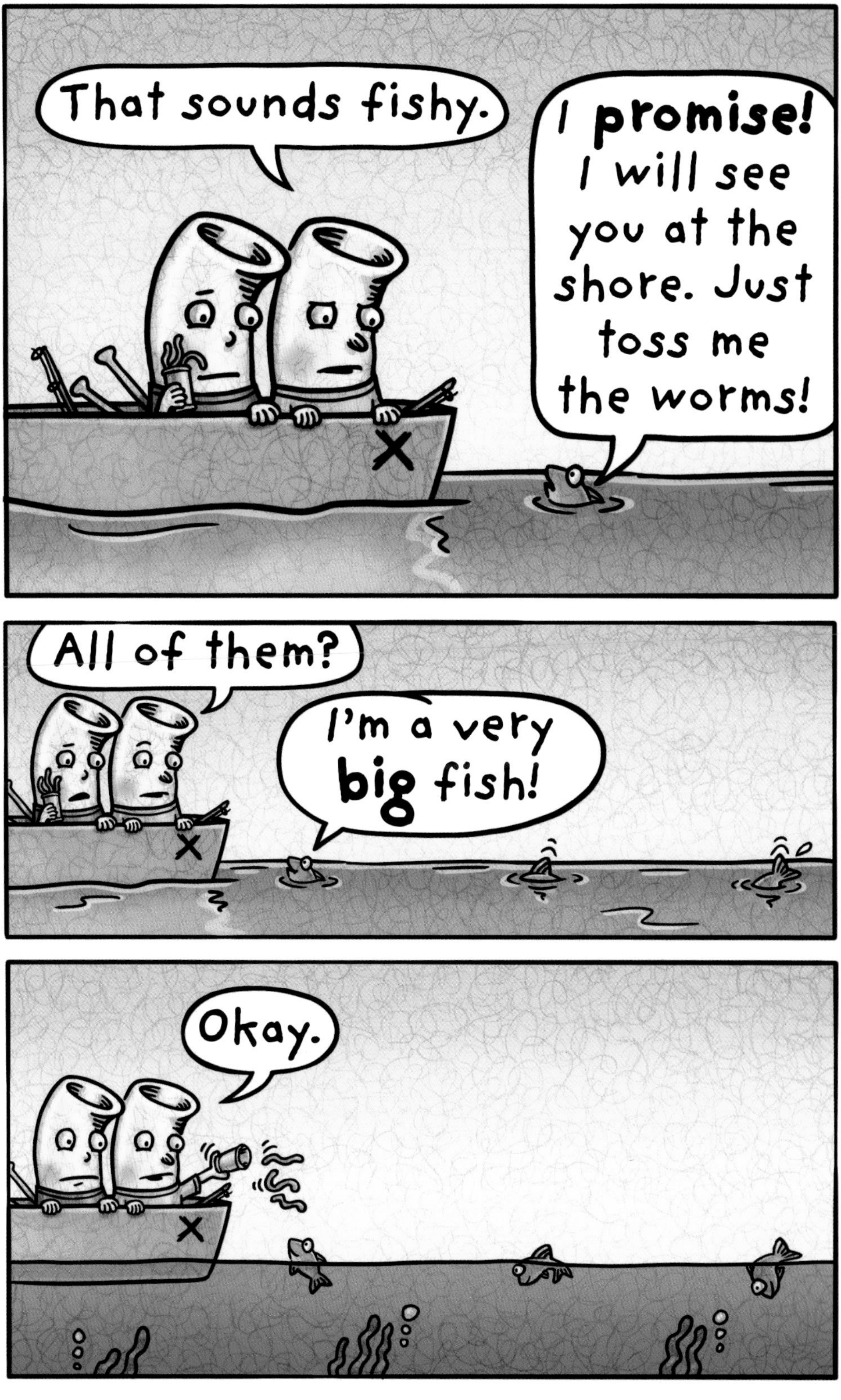
That sounds fishy.
I **promise!** I will see you at the shore. Just toss me the worms!
All of them?
I'm a very **big** fish!
Okay.

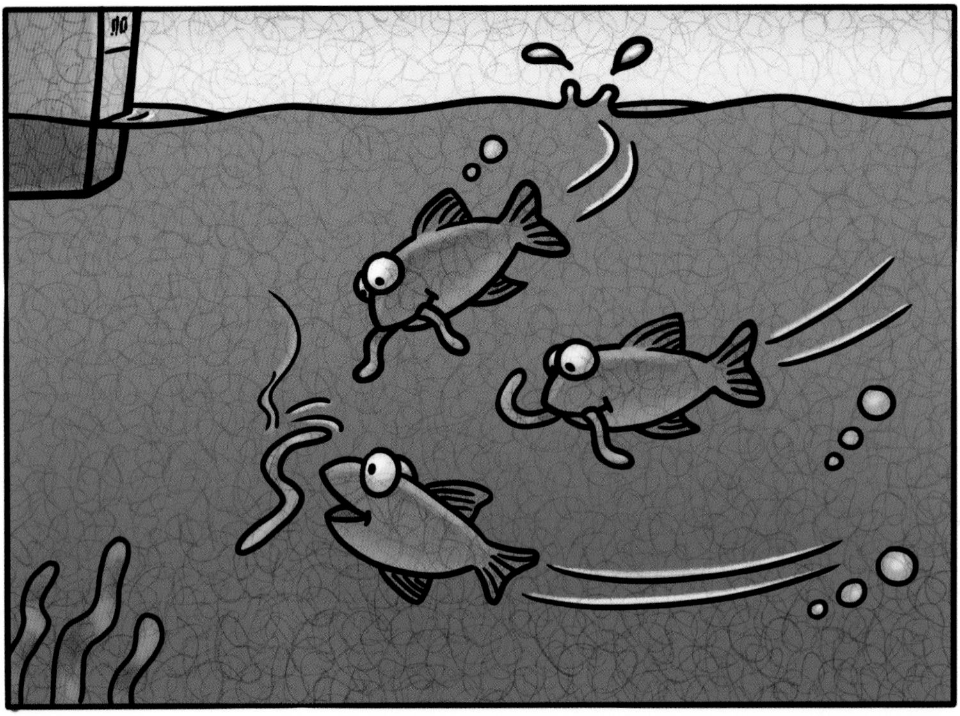

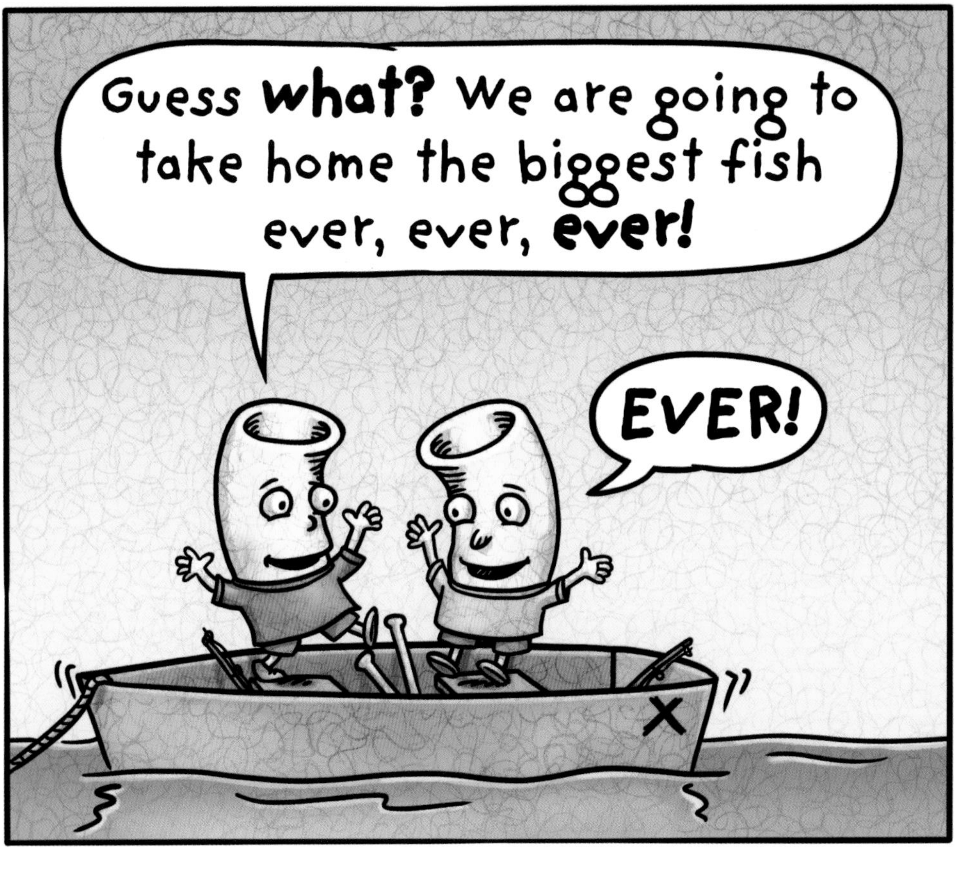
Guess what? We are going to take home the biggest fish ever, ever, ever!
EVER!

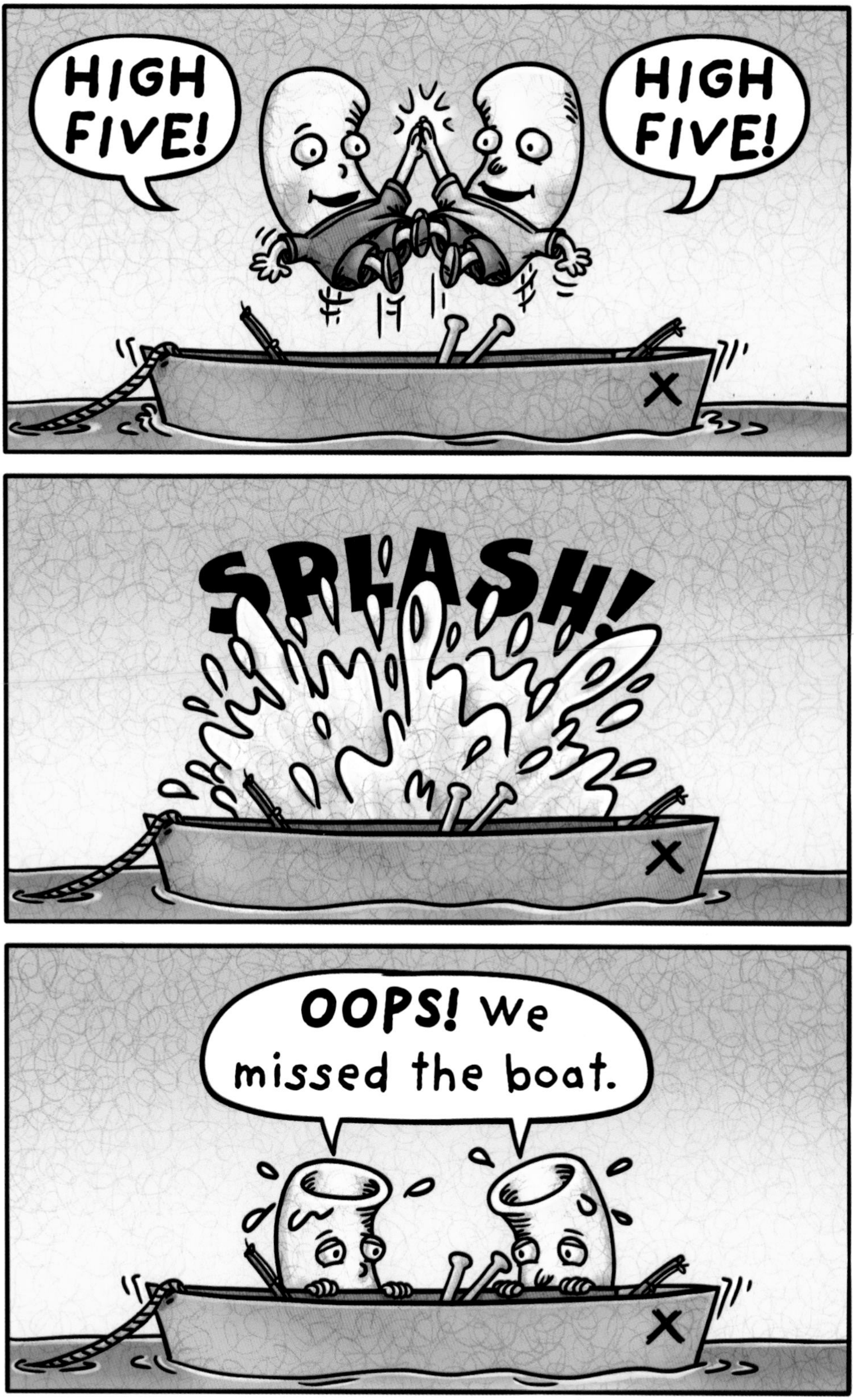
HIGH FIVE!
HIGH FIVE!
SPLASH!
OOPS! We missed the boat.

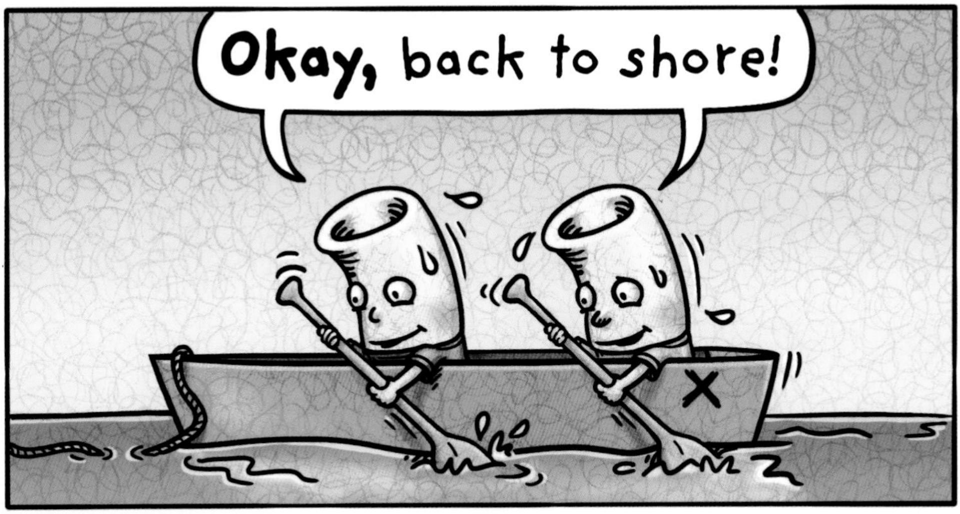
Okay, back to shore!
X

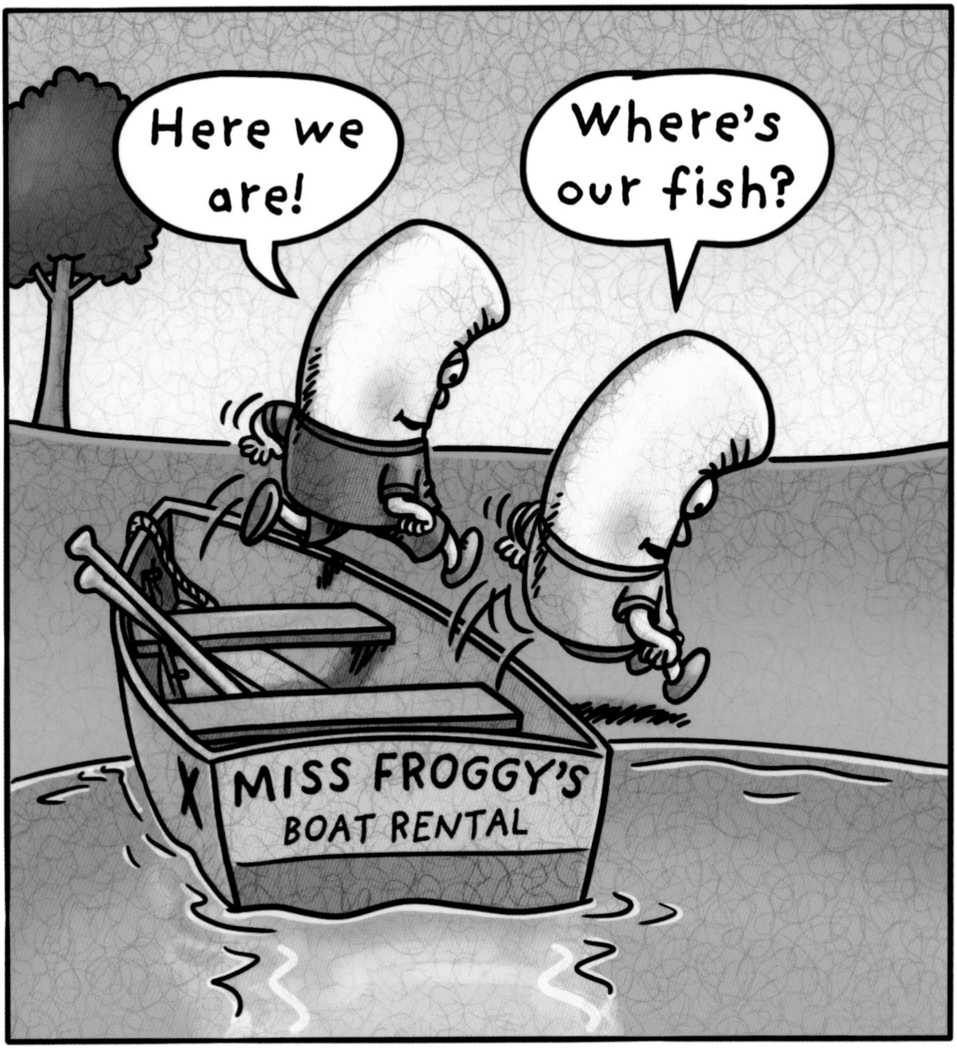
Here we are!
Where's our fish?
X
MISS FROGGY'S BOAT RENTAL

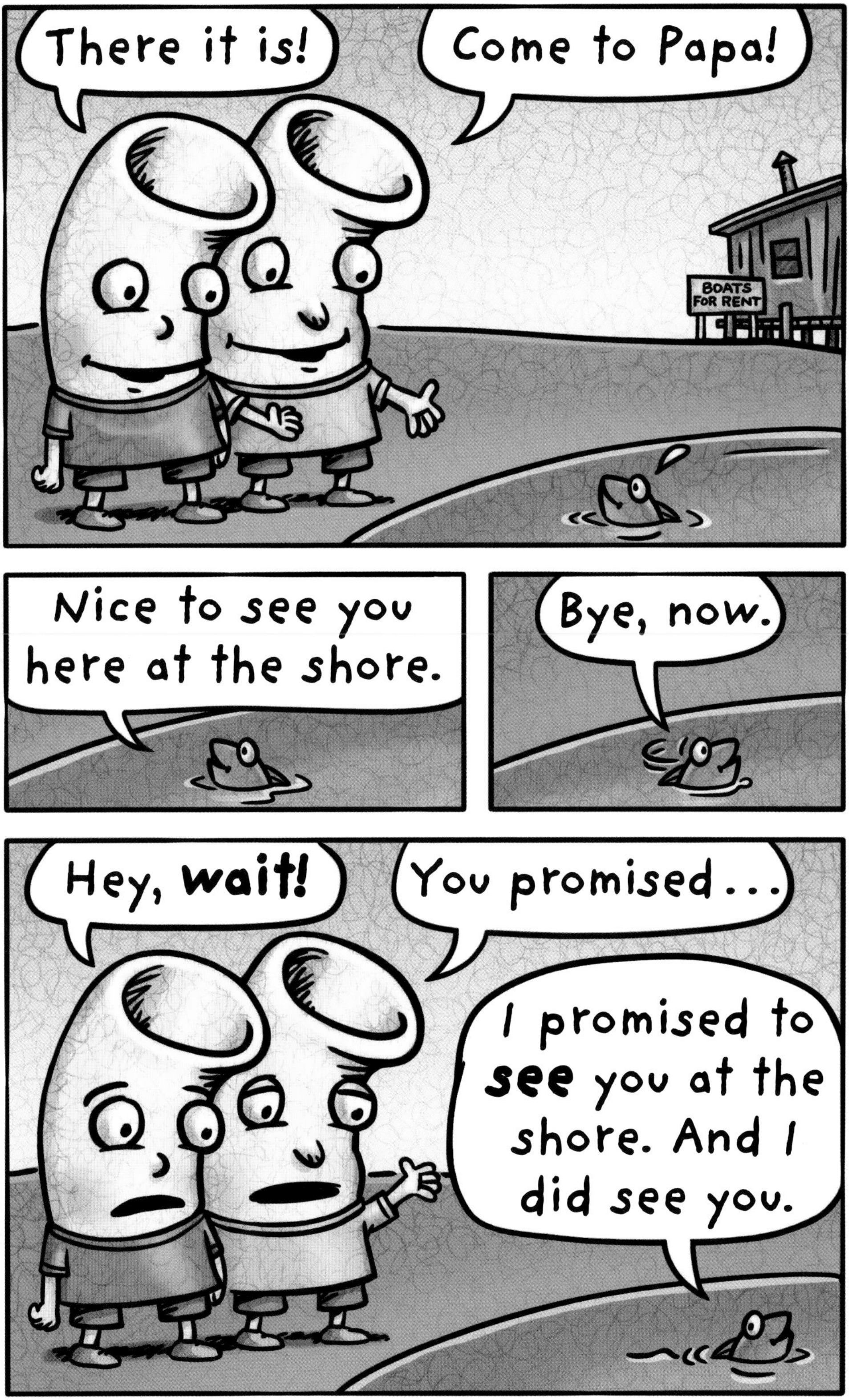
There it is!
Come to Papa!
BOATS FOR RENT
Nice to see you here at the shore.
Bye, now.
Hey, **wait!**
You promised...
I promised to **see** you at the shore. And I did see you.

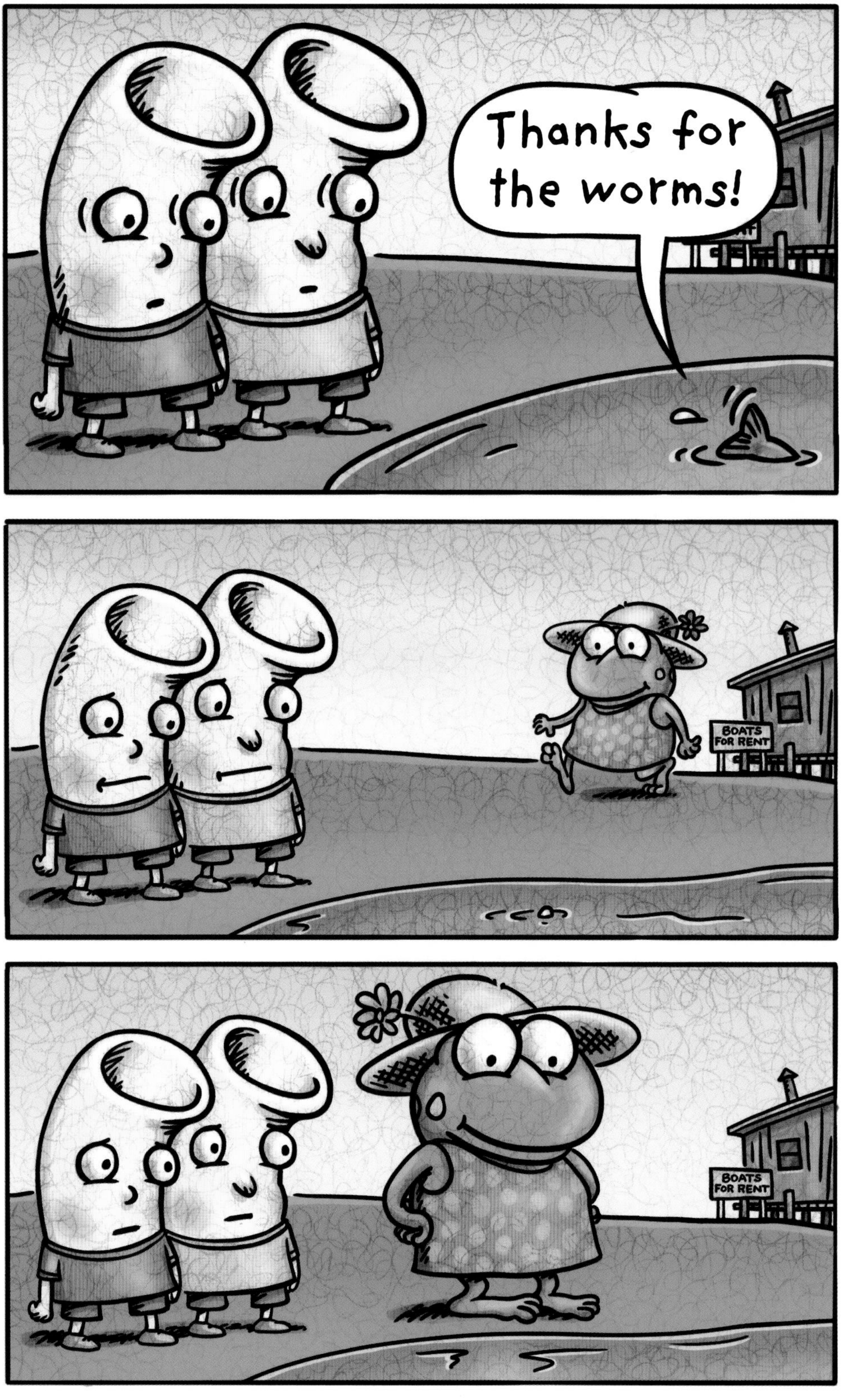
Thanks for the worms!
BOATS FOR RENT
BOATS FOR RENT

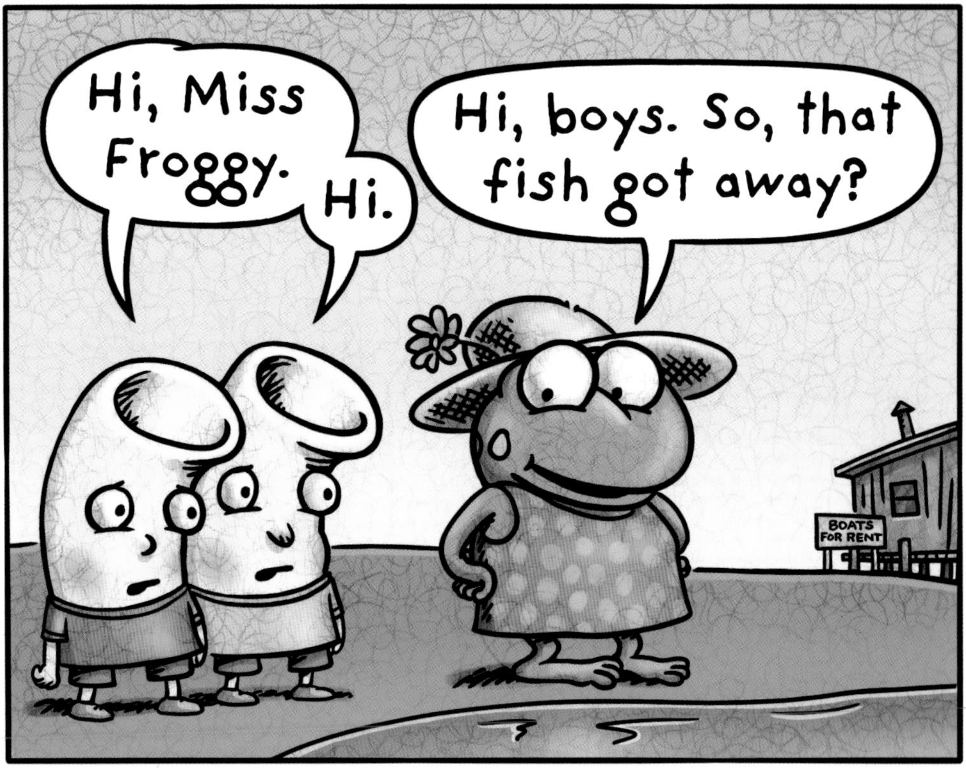
Hi, Miss Froggy.
Hi.
Hi, boys. So, that fish got away?
BOATS FOR RENT

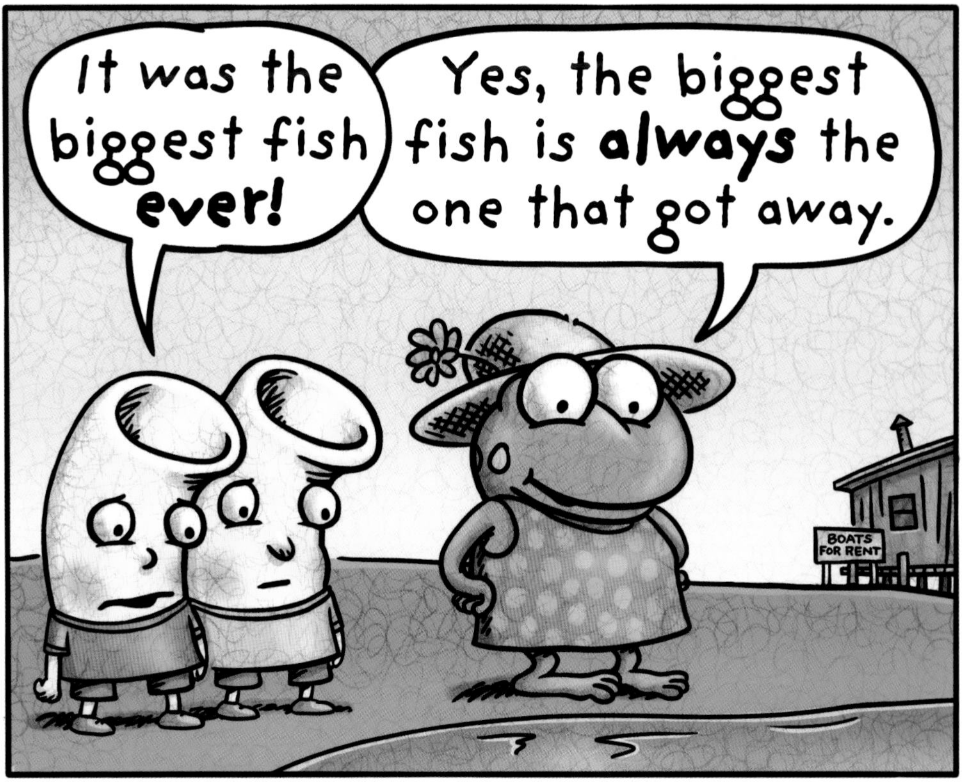
It was the biggest fish **ever!**
Yes, the biggest fish is **always** the one that got away.
BOATS FOR RENT

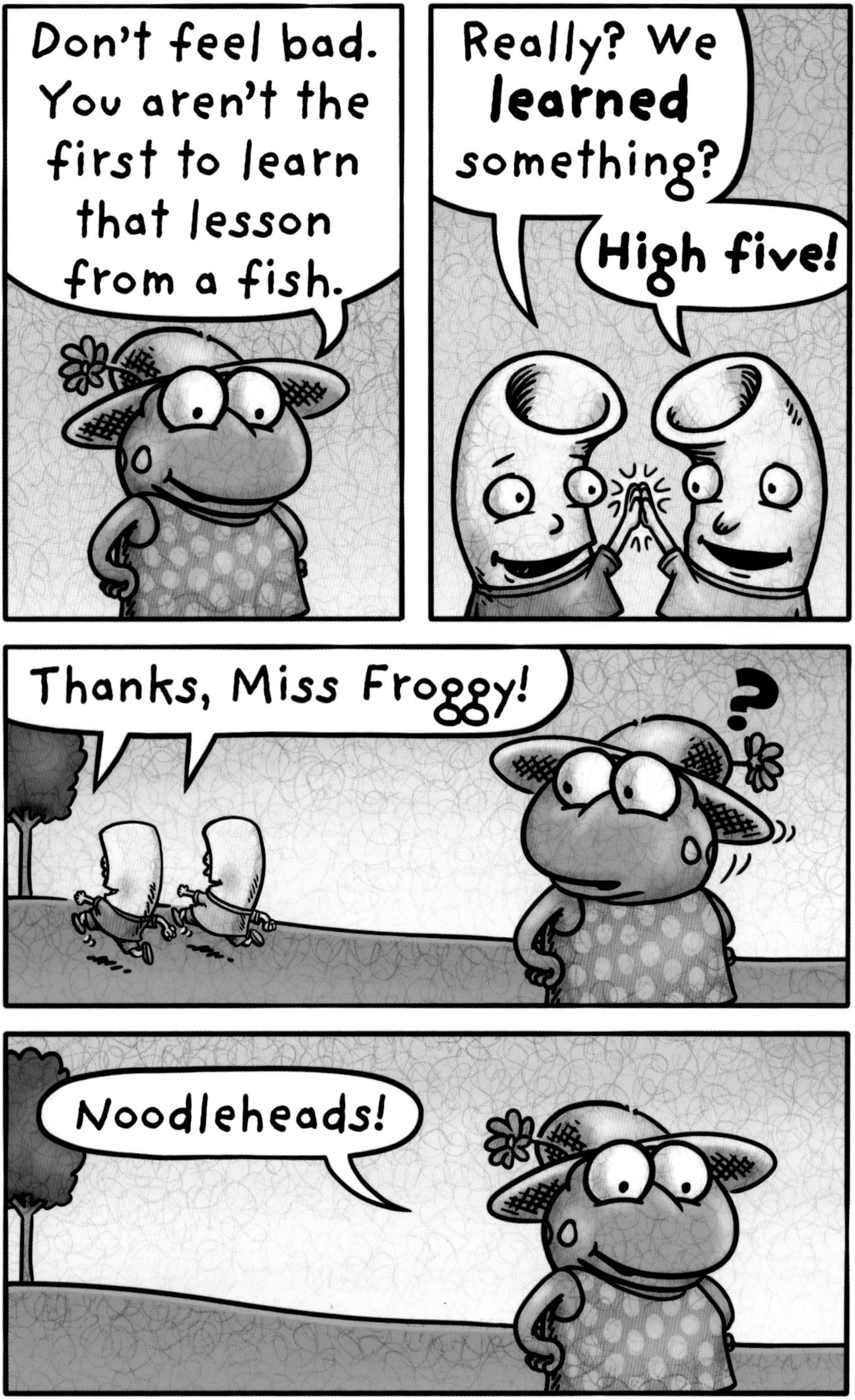
Don't feel bad. You aren't the first to learn that lesson from a fish.
Really? We **learned** something?
High five!
Thanks, Miss Froggy!
?
Noodleheads!

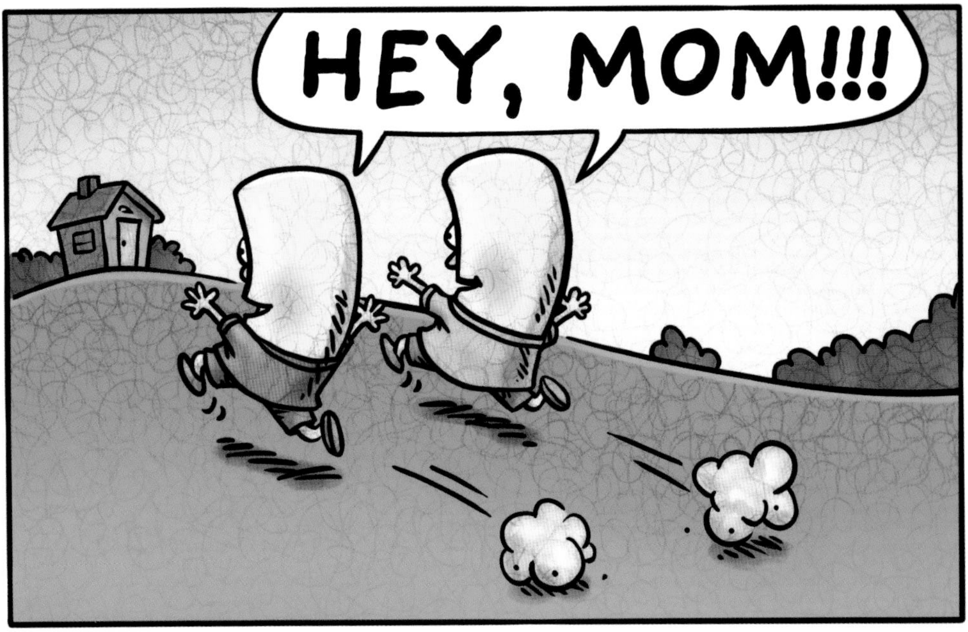
HEY, MOM!!!

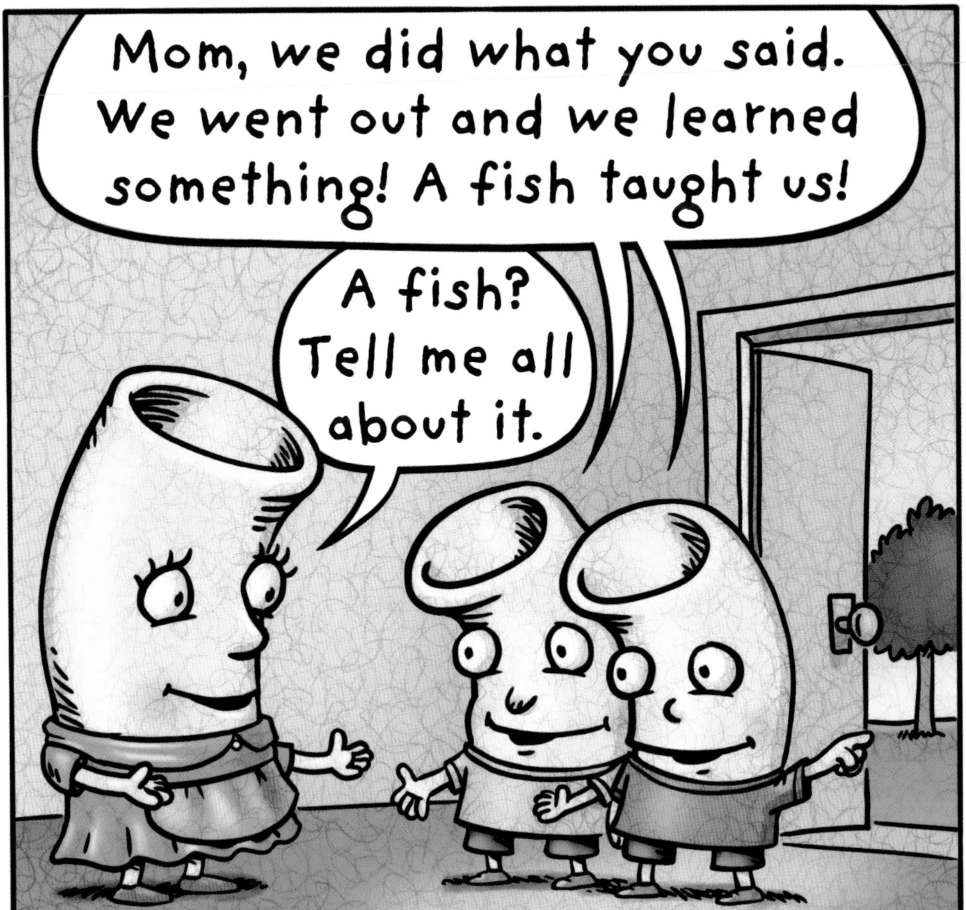
Mom, we did what you said. We went out and we learned something! A fish taught us!
A fish? Tell me all about it.

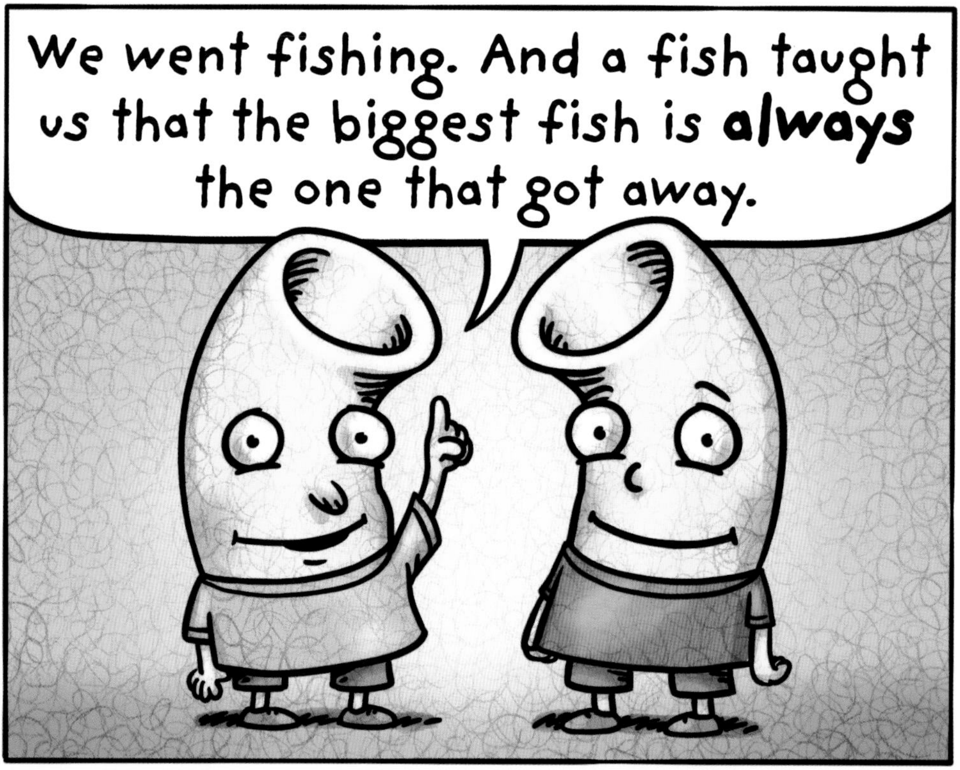
We went fishing. And a fish taught us that the biggest fish is **always** the one that got away.

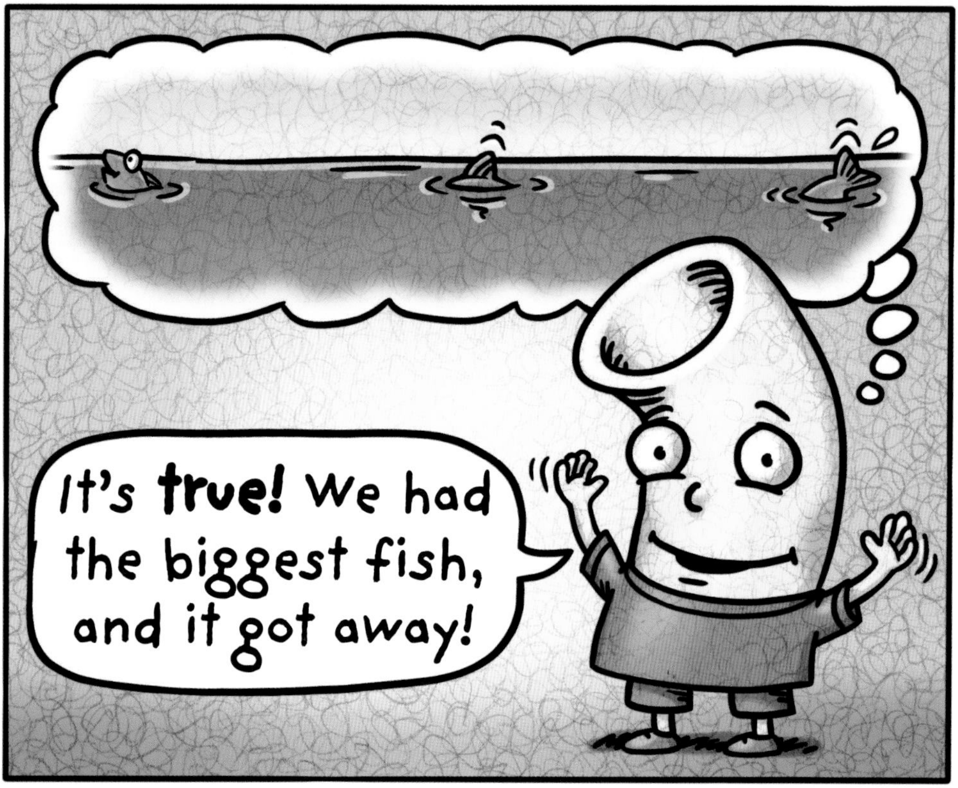
It's **true!** We had the biggest fish, and it got away!

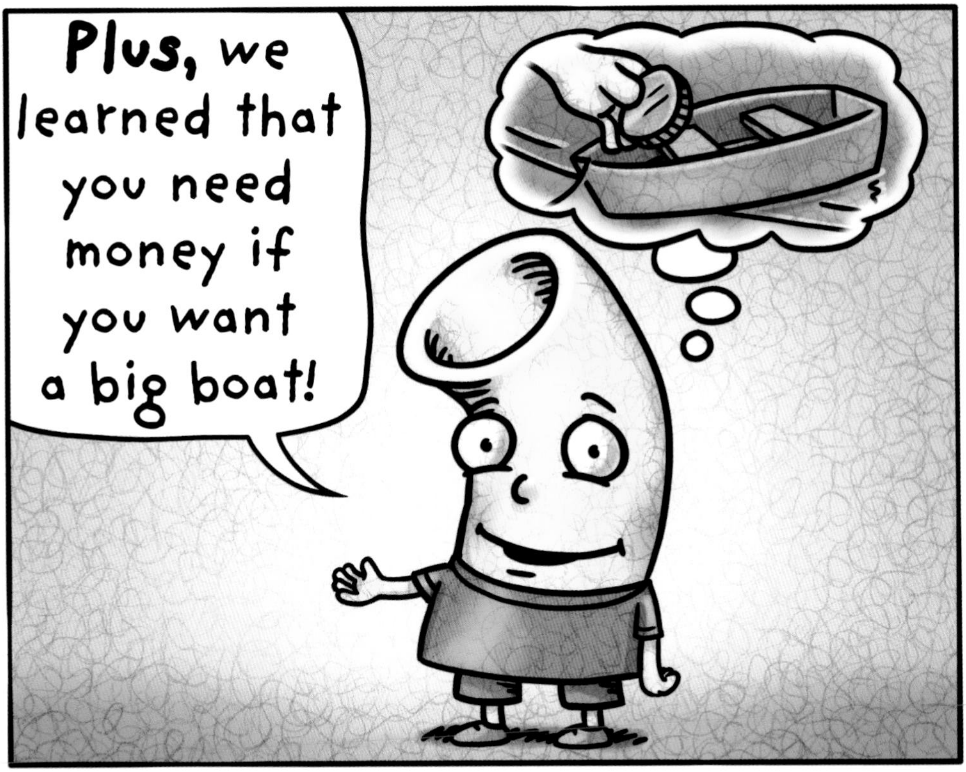
Plus, we learned that you need money if you want a big boat!

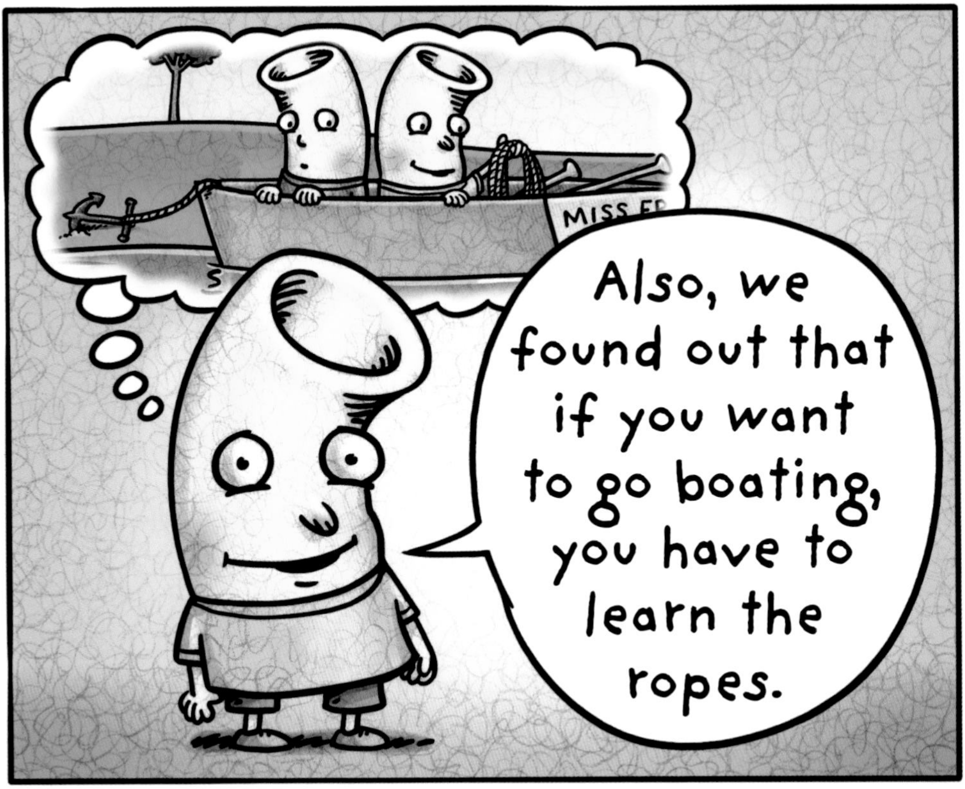
MISS FR
Also, we found out that if you want to go boating, you have to learn the ropes.

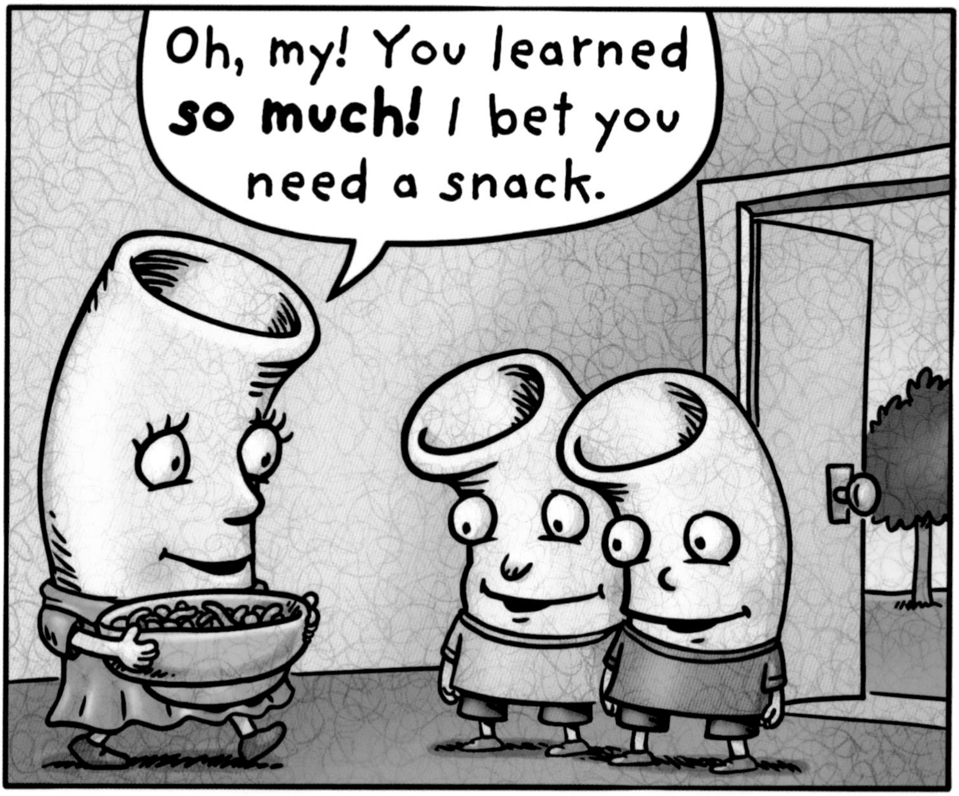
Oh, my! You learned **so much!** I bet you need a snack.

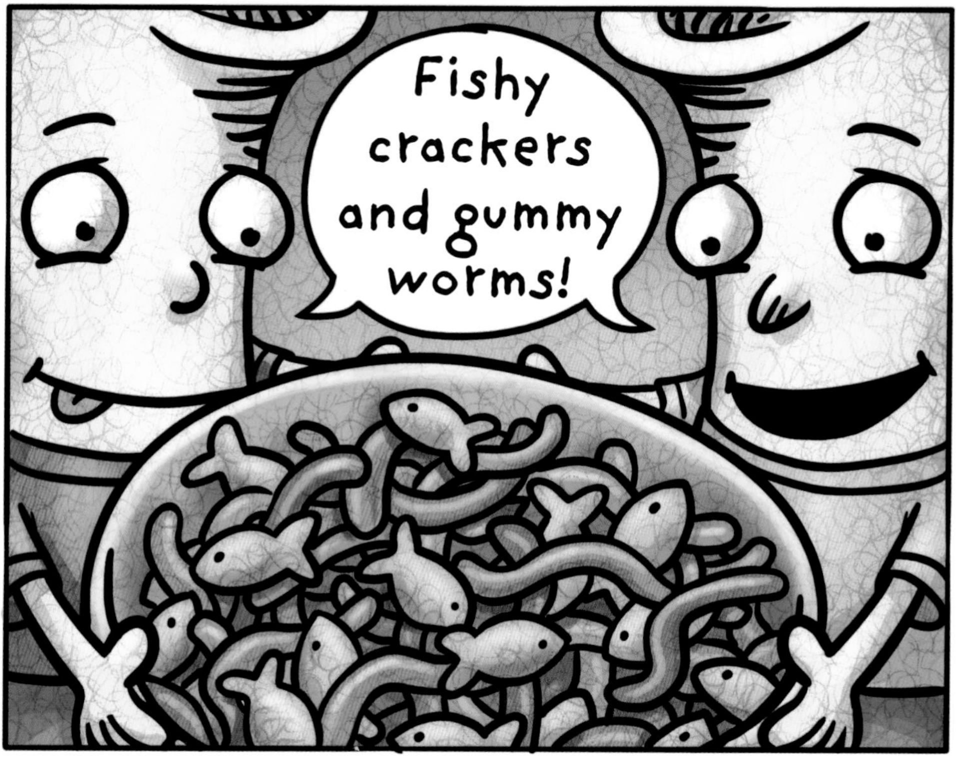
Fishy crackers and gummy worms!

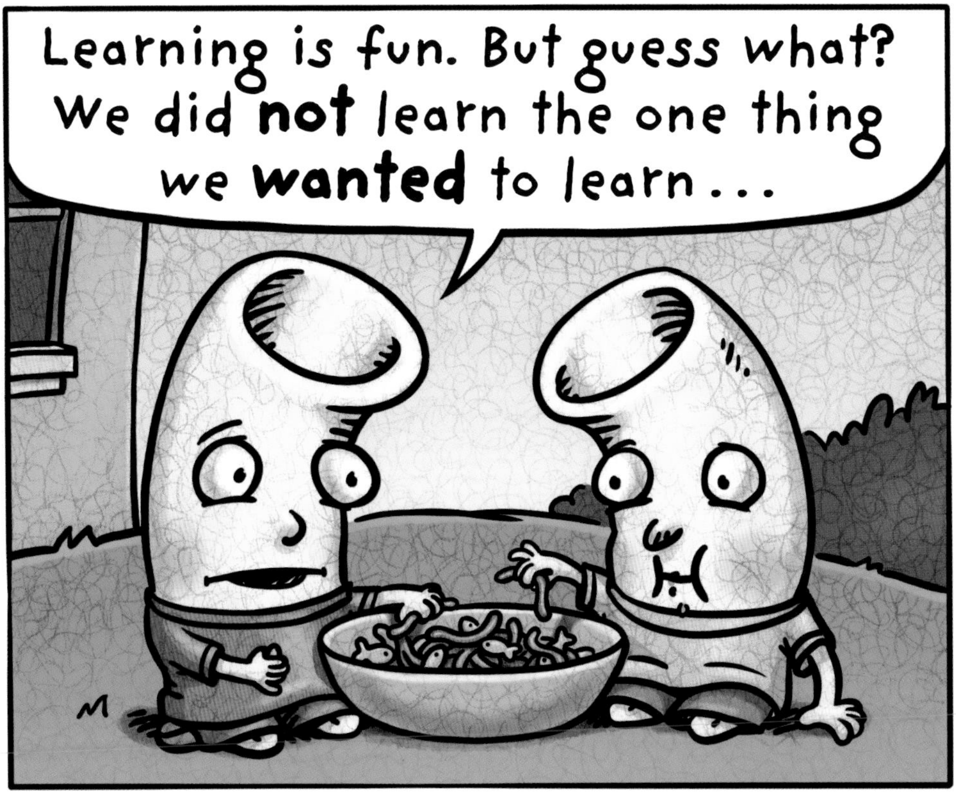
Learning is fun. But guess what? We did **not** learn the one thing we **wanted** to learn . . .

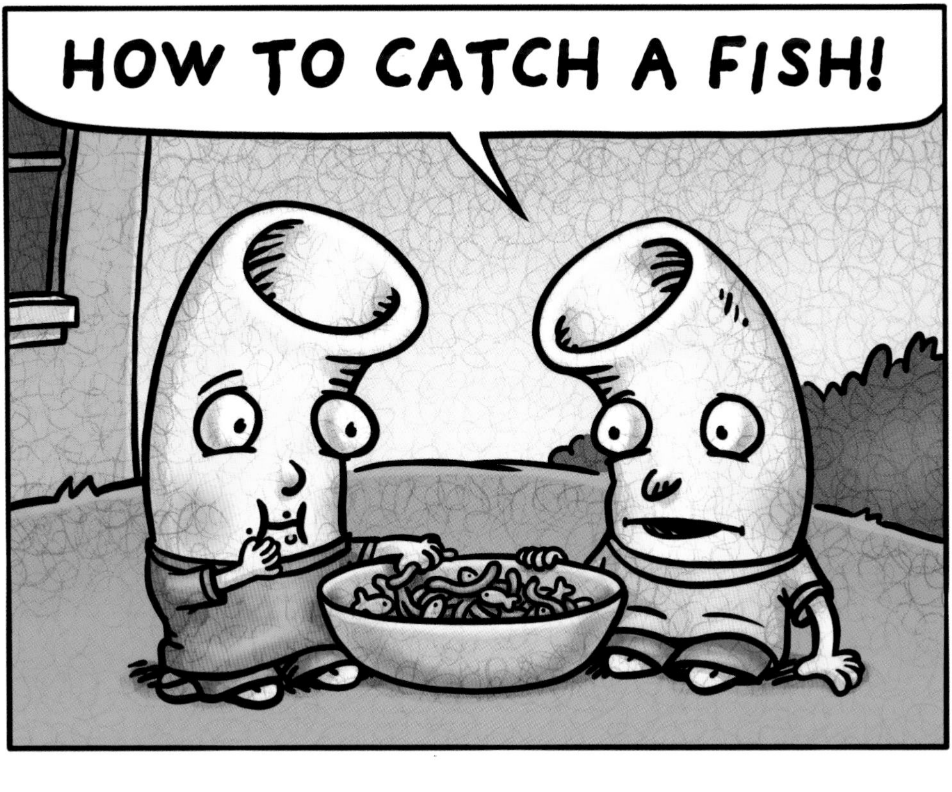
HOW TO CATCH A FISH!

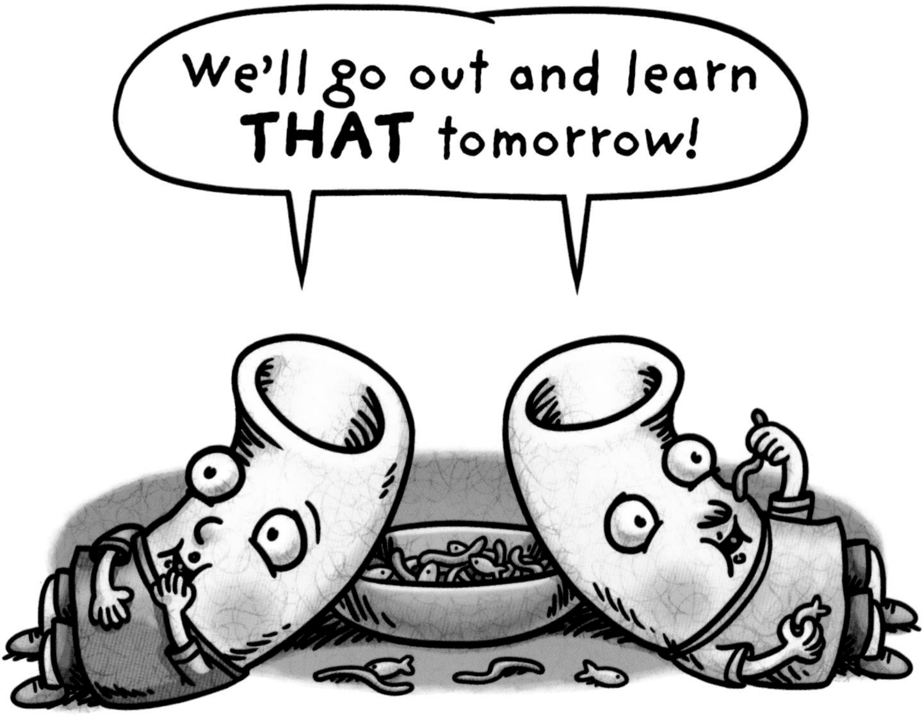
We'll go out and learn
THAT tomorrow!

Authors' Notes

Story Sources for Noodleheads Find Something Fishy

Everyone has done something foolish at one time or another. As a result, tales of fools, also called "noodles" or "noodleheads," have been told for as long as people have told stories. In 1888, W. A. Clouston wrote a scholarly book called *The Book of Noodles* in which he described numerous stories that had been told for hundreds of years, and quite a few dating back more than two millennia. We have used these old stories as inspiration for Mac and Mac's adventures. People around the world tell similar stories about their particular fools, such as Giufà in Italy, Nasreddin Hodja in Turkey, Juan Bobo in Puerto Rico, and Jack in England. The expression "Fortune, that favors fools" is apt, for, in spite of their foolishness, things usually turn out fine in the end for the fool. Perhaps this is because they are generally kind and well-meaning. Noodlehead stories help children to understand humor and logical thinking; kids quickly see that noodleheads are totally illogical—usually to an absurd extent.

The motifs to which we refer in the information that follows are from *The Storyteller's Sourcebook: A Subject, Title, and Motif Index to Folklore Collections for Children* by Margaret Read MacDonald, 1st edition (Detroit: Gale, 1982) and 2nd edition (Detroit: Gale, 2001). Tale types are from *A Guide to Folktales in the English Language* by D. L. Ashliman (NY: Greenwood, 1987).

Introduction

The motif in this section is J2171.6.2, Potter cannot get pole through gate. In Lee Wyndham's *Tales People Tell in China* (NY: Messner, 1970, p. 64), a pottery maker, hoping to sell his pots in a nearby town, puts them in two nets, ties the nets to the ends of a bamboo pole, and carries the pole on his shoulders. He can't, however, figure out how to get the long pole through the town gate. First the potter carries the pole horizontally, and the gate is too narrow. Then he holds it vertically, and the gate is too low. A wise bystander notices and advises the potter to carry it lengthwise or sideways. In another variant found in *Sweet and Sour: Tales from China* by Carol Kendall and Yao-wen Li (NY: Seabury, 1978, pp. 45–48), the town magistrate is named Old Fuddlement because of his lack of common sense. When a fool, or "muddlehead," as a fool is called in this town, makes the same mistake as the potter, Old Fuddlement's silly advice is, "Why didn't you saw the pole in two? You could have been home in bed by now!"

Chapter 1: How to Grow a Boat

The motif in this chapter is J2212.7*, Boat expected to grow into a ship. The inspiration came from "The Little Boat" in Lillian Bason's collection *Those Foolish Molboes!* (NY: Cowan, McCann & Geoghegan, 1977). In Denmark, they tell stories of an entire village of fools who live on the peninsula of Mols and are known as the Molboes. This is Denmark's equivalent to the Jewish village of Chelm in Poland, or Gotham in England. In the story, several Molboes travel to a big city on the coast where they are impressed by one of the large ships in the harbor. They cannot afford a big ship but purchase a small one that they hope will grow in time. Alas, despite their best efforts, the little boat never becomes a big ship. The captain who sells the small boat to the Molboes takes advantage of their gullibility, as Meatball does with Mac and Mac. Noodlehead stories make children aware that they should not believe everything they hear. The expression "sounds fishy" means that something seems to be dishonest or suspicious. It originated when fishermen tried to convince customers that old fish were fresh, in spite of the smell.

Chapter 2: Finding Fish

This story was inspired by "The Foolish Fisherman" in Florence Botsford's *Picture Tales from the Italian* (Philadelphia: J. B. Lippincott, 1929, pp. 13–14). After a crew of fishermen rows all night without getting anywhere, the captain is convinced that the boat is bewitched. Someone finally notices that they are still tied to the dock. The solution of the longer rope was our own idea. Uh-oh! We are starting to think like noodleheads!

The motif of marking the boat (J1922.1, Marking the place on the boat) seems to have made its way around the world. It is tale type 1278, Marking the boat. We found many examples, including an Irish version in W. A. Clouston's *The Book of Noodles* (London: Elliot Stock, 1888, p. 99); a Danish version in Lillian Bason's *Those Foolish Molboes!* (NY: Cowan, McCann & Geoghegan, 1977, pp. 36–47); and a Chinese variant in Lee Wyndham's *Tales People Tell in China* (NY: Messner, 1970, p. 66).

Chapter 3: The Biggest Fish

The inspiration for this story came from the common motif K11.1, Race won by deception: relative helpers, where a slower animal gets relatives to station them-selves at intervals in the line of a race in order to fool a faster animal. Although a race is not involved here, the concept is the same. Among the many versions we found a German variant in Wanda Gág's *More Tales from Grimm* (NY: Coward-McCann, 1947, pp. 163–170); an English version in Walter de la Mare's *Animal Stories* (NY: Scribner, 1939, pp. 3–8); and an African American version in Harold Courlander's *Terrapin's Pot of Sense* (NY: Holt, 1957, pp. 28–30). It is also tale type 275A*, The race between the hedgehog and the hare.

When Mac and Mac high-five each other, they literally "miss the boat" and fall into the water. The expression "miss the boat" began in the time before airplanes and cars when most people traveled by boat. It is also used figuratively to mean that one has missed out on an opportunity.

The phrase "learn the ropes" originated in the days of sailing ships, before they were powered by steam or fossil fuels. A new sailor would begin by learning how to tie knots and control the ropes attached to the sails in order to help the ship catch the wind. Today, of course, "learn the ropes" is used to describe learning the basics of any job.